The Best British Short Stories 2012

NICHOLAS ROYLE is the author of more than 100 short stories, two novellas and six novels. His short story collection, *Mortality* (Serpent's Tail), was shortlisted for the inaugural Edge Hill Prize. He has edited fifteen anthologies of short stories, including *A Book of Two Halves* (Gollancz), *The Time Out Book of Paris Short Stories* (Penguin), *'68: New Stories by Children of the Revolution* (Salt) and *Murmurations: An Anthology of Uncanny Stories About Birds* (Two Ravens Press). A senior lecturer in creative writing at the Manchester Writing School at MMU, he reviews fiction for the *Independent* and the *Warwick Review*. A new novel, *First Novel* (Jonathan Cape), is due to appear in 2013 and a collection of short stories, *London Labyrinth* (No Exit Press), is forthcoming. He lives in Manchester. He also runs Nightjar Press, publishing original short stories as signed, limited-edition chapbooks.

Also by Nicholas Royle:

NOVELS
Counterparts
Saxophone Dreams
The Matter of the Heart
The Director's Cut
Antwerp
Regicide

NOVELLAS
The Appetite
The Enigma of Departure

SHORT STORIES
Mortality

ANTHOLOGIES (as editor)
Darklands
Darklands 2
A Book of Two Halves
The Tiger Garden: A Book of Writers' Dreams
The Time Out Book of New York Short Stories
The Ex Files: New Stories About Old Flames
The Agony & the Ecstasy: New Writing for the World Cup
Neonlit: Time Out Book of New Writing
The Time Out Book of Paris Short Stories
Neonlit: Time Out Book of New Writing Volume 2
The Time Out Book of London Short Stories Volume 2
Dreams Never End
'68: New Stories From Children of the Revolution
The Best British Short Stories 2011
Murmurations: An Anthology of Uncanny Stories About Birds

The Best British Short Stories 2012

edited by

NICHOLAS ROYLE

SALT

LONDON

PUBLISHED BY SALT PUBLISHING

Acre House, 12-15 William Road, London NW1 3ER United Kingdom

Selection and introduction © Nicholas Royle, 2012
Individual contributions © the Contributors

Printed in Great Britain by Clays Ltd, St Ives plc

Typeset in Bembo 12 / 13.5

ISBN 978 1 90773 18 1 paperback

1 3 5 7 9 8 6 4 2

To the memory of William Sansom (1912–76)

Contents

Introduction

I T W A S O N L Y when I came to write this introduction – always the last task – that it dawned on me: this year's selection might seem a rather dark one. It wasn't deliberate; there was no plan. But, still, for every dead body you have to step over, there's a moment of emotional uplift. Well, maybe not *every* dead body. Let's face it, death casts a long shadow. But it's precisely because of our knowledge of our mortality that we feel compelled to live our lives to the full. Isn't it?

The other thing I noticed, and this I noticed while I was still choosing the stories, is that there is no crossover with last year's volume. None of the writers included in the 2011 anthology is featured in this one. This, again, was not deliberate. I was tempted by new stories I came across by David Rose, Kirsty Logan and Philip Langeskov, as well as by a great many stories by other writers that were good enough to be considered among the best published last year, but competition is fierce.

I am aware also, looking at the contents page, that there are thirteen stories by men writers and only seven by women. I say 'men writers' to point up the absurdity and offensiveness of a term in wide general use – 'women writers'. Again, not deliberate; maybe I should be bothered by the imbalance, but in all honesty I'm not. Maybe next year's volume will go the other way, maybe it won't. I'm suspicious of quotas. I read as widely as I could during the year and these twenty stories are, in my opinion, the best I saw, irrespective of gender, race, region – yes, region; I couldn't care less about religion – or any other variable.

The 2011 anthology contained three stories from the *Warwick Review*, an excellent magazine that faced a funding crisis towards the end of last year. As I write, it has just had funding approved, but only until the summer. I very much hope the magazine will survive beyond the end of the university year and go on to publish many more good stories. Had I been allowed to include twenty-one stories in this book instead of twenty, I would have sought to include 'Time Management' by Kathryn Simmonds, which appeared in the March 2011 issue of the *Warwick Review*.

But, I didn't, and I'm very pleased with the choices I have made. I could not be more aware that this is a personal selection and another editor would come up with an entirely different list. Readers will agree with some choices and disagree with others and that's fine. Let's talk about which are the *best* stories being published. It beats talking about whether the form is alive or dead. Let's hope we're beyond that dreary debate. Of course the short story is in good health – in excellent health, in fact. This book is dedicated to the memory of William Sansom, a great, idiosyncratic short story writer and highly individual prose stylist, born a hundred years ago last month. There are writers in this book who can make the hairs stand up on the back of my neck in the same way he could. Not by being scary – although some can do that as well, as indeed Sansom could – but by creating the delicious tension you feel when you know you are reading a good writer, someone totally in control of their material, someone who understands that the most important words are not those on the page, but those left out, those left for the reader to fill in.

Three of these stories brought on the waterworks. A couple more delivered a well-aimed emotional punch. One or two had me grinning with delight at their sheer cleverness and invention. They all embody the unexpected (without being *Tales of the Unexpected*). One of the darkest stories here is also one of the funniest. Two stories are about libraries and those stories, which open and close the book, are both from the excellent *Paraxis*, an online magazine edited by Claire Massey, Andy Hedgecock and Carys Bray. Their second volume took the library as its theme. Like many children of my generation, I haunted libraries. I discovered things in libraries, I learned to question things in libraries, I fell in love in libraries.

In this country, at the time of writing, four hundred public libraries face the threat of closure.

But things change. The financial situation. Public opinion. Even governments, eventually.

In the meantime, the natural human desire to be told stories will remain as strong as it ever was – and here are twenty of the best.

— NICHOLAS ROYLE
Manchester
February 2012

EMMA JANE UNSWORTH

I Arrive First

THAT MEANS IT is my turn to start. I put my cloth bag down on the table and make my way over to the shelves. I walk past Poetry towards General Fiction and move along the rows, tapping a few spines as I go. I finally settle on Tom Wolfe, *The Bonfire of the Vanities*. The book is hard-backed, big and heavy. When it comes off the shelf it leaves a wide gap that the surrounding books domino-fall into. I carry it in both hands back across the room. I lost my hairbrush this morning. I turned the bathroom inside out looking for it but it was no good; it's gone for ever. The best I could do was drag my fingers through my hair and scrape it back into a snarly bun. I position the book in the usual place: upside down in the top right corner of the table. It's a tenuous joke but I know he'll get it. We're on the same wavelength.

I pull my netbook and papers out of my bag and stand my bottle of water on my left-hand side, lining it up with the *exact* centre of my netbook. Then I sit back, ready. He won't be long. It's got to the point where I can almost sense him approaching, like a cat that knows when its owner's car will turn into the drive.

Other students arrive. They swing through the doors

and then whisper and scatter throughout the library. Some of them slip into the clinically lit catacombs that radiate from the central hub. I look up to the bright-stained dome in the roof and watch the shafts of light fall and flash over the cells of the curved perimeter wall, making everything gleam with life. A trolley of returned books waits by the lending desk and a librarian pats the handle and then pushes off in the direction of social sciences, wheeling the trolley across the room like it's a buggy with a baby in it. The trolley and the librarian disappear amongst the rows of shelves and I tap my fingers on the mousepad of my netbook and type a few words to pass the time. This is what I write:

The library is due to close for refurbishment in one week.

No sooner have I typed it than a few of the hairs on my right arm rear up off my skin and I know he's coming through the door. I don't know what gives it away to my outer senses – whether it's the way his feet fall or the first scent-flares of his deodorant – but it's like I've got a special kind of radar where he's concerned. He puts his bag on the desk gently, oh so gently, and then he stands there for a moment, still and softly posed in the full quiet of the library. My eyes flick on him and past him, on him and past him; past him when he looks my way and then on him again when he looks up, and I look up with him for a moment, up to the dome that is now splitting rays of sun through its antique glass, filling the air with buttery light. I see that he is wearing a green shirt and is holding a scrap of paper in his hand.

He must have seen it by now.

As he walks to the shelves he pretends to scrutinise the scrap of paper in his hand but I know this is all just

5

part of today's elaborate faux nonchalance. He's thinking, considering the options, like I was just a few minutes ago. He takes his time – ten minutes almost – and I tap away on my netbook while I watch him.

I don't know where we're all going to go.

I don't, and that's the truth. Me and him. The books. The librarians. The birds that drip from the ledges outside. Should we scatter to different corners of the city; the world? Or should we meet in condensation-lined coffee shops and measure out the days in little wooden sticks?

He has a book. He brings it back. I let it sit. Him sit. I don't look for at least two minutes according to the digital clock in the corner of my screen. Then I glance at the book and away, at the book and away. It's enough. I see it. *The Line of Beauty.* What a charmer. He looks past me then at me then past me again. A wide, grey, ambiguous look. I touch my cheek, my forehead; I slide my fingers along my scraped back hair and needle a ratty bump beneath the surface with my nail.

It's been going on for a month now. The first time, *One Hundred Years of Solitude* just sitting there in front of him, upside down, as he worked. You couldn't miss it. Well, you obviously could miss it, because plenty of people hadn't noticed it at all. From what I could tell no one else in the library was replying. I looked around at the other students working at tables, scanning for another book laid out that way. Nada. It was incredible to me that such a cry for help, for attention, for contact, was being ignored. But that's the way it is with wavelengths and thank god for that, because if everyone was on the same wavelength you wouldn't be able to make out a thing over the din. He looked up from his work and I looked down to his trainers under the table and saw they were done up so tightly that the eyelets almost met. When I looked up again he smiled at me and I smiled back and nodded to the book and he kept smiling and there was something about the angle of his mouth that was like the angle of the book. And the table opposite was free so I sat down and thought of how best to reply. As I saw it, there was only one option, and it was sure to be on the shelf, under D, a short walk away: *Rebecca*. My name.

I always notice what people are reading. Whenever I'm on a bus or a train and see someone reading I strain to see what it is. Some people don't like it – they cover their (book) protectively with their hands, afraid of what it might reveal. Other people proudly hold their BOOKS out in front of them – these are usually the same books: the latest must-read, or Don DeLillo's *Underworld*. But you can tell so much by what someone has chosen, and I'd be coy about it too, if I didn't mean everything the book in front of me said – on the outside, because that's what counts. The insides of books don't interest me any more.

I still wonder how long he had been laying that book out, waiting for an answer. I think that will be one of my first questions, when we eventually speak. A week, that's all we have left now.

Will we make some kind of plan, or will that ruin everything?

At quarter to five we pack up, as usual. They don't kick out until six but I think we both like to be ahead of the rush.

The next day I panic because someone is sitting at my table. This has happened before, but now that time is of the essence I can't stop myself from panicking and have to go to the Ladies and run cold water over my wrists. He's there at his table already but I haven't had chance to see what he's put out yet.

When I come out from the toilet the first thing I do is check that the person in my seat hasn't started talking to him instead. I see with relief that she hasn't. There is nothing on the table apart from a magazine. I hope this means that she won't be long. I linger to one side of her table, willing her away. She looks up at me and I stare hard, meaningfully, but it's no good, she doesn't understand. She's not on my wavelength. I step away towards the next table, but before I sit down I look over at his book. *After You'd Gone*, Maggie O'Farrell. Brilliant, just brilliant. I sit down feeling calmer and take out my netbook and type a few words while I'm waiting for the girl to move.

This place will be spooky when it's empty.

The girl folds up her magazine and noisily reverses her chair. I snap my netbook shut and grab my bag and am in her seat two seconds after she has vacated it. She tuts as she walks away but I ignore her. I breathe deeply and feel as though everything is all right now. He hasn't looked up once during the changeover and I wonder whether he will swap the book or whether it is up to me to go and find one. I wait five minutes.

Like a church on a weekday.

Then he gets up and goes towards the shelves, leaving the book where it is. What does this mean? A double message? Will he use two titles to make a sentence? That would be a first.

Things have to progress, I suppose.

He is back quickly. As he emerges from the shelves he almost collides with a moving trolley but swerves in a balletic move to avoid a crash and smiles at the librarian, although I can't see whether the librarian is smiling back. I smile at him but he doesn't look over and he is empty-handed. What does this mean? But as he sits down something beautiful happens: the bulb in the lamp on his table pops and dies. He grimaces and I can tell he is considering moving, he looks up at the dome, at the surrounding lights, and I feel the panic rising in my stomach again but then he shrugs and sits back down. This is a chance now, surely. I leap to my feet and power-walk along the shelves to S. I can't get back to my seat quick enough, can't wait for him to see how good this one is. I would run if it wasn't inappropriate to run across a library. I land in my seat and the book skids into position on the table. *The Dark Room*, Rachel Seiffert. It's almost as good as when the heating hadn't caught up with the season and he put out *Love in a Cold Climate*. I fizzed at his wit while the word **LOVE** blazed off the dustjacket in my direction.

Over the next two days we take things up another notch. He arrives first both mornings. Is he implying I should start arriving earlier too, in order to maximise our time together?

We're running out.

On the third-to-last day he pores over a marked essay. I can't see the exact mark but I presume it's not very good because the book he has chosen is *The Scarlet Letter*. The mark on the essay might be in pencil, but I can read between the lines.

The following afternoon a group of schoolchildren come for a tour and they bang into tables and pull faces and shout, despite their supervisor telling them to shush. I put out *Animal Farm*. He replies with Atwood: *Alias Grace*. He's right of course. We were all there once. I try not to let the kids rile me after that even though I am uncomfortable because I rushed my lunchtime banana.

I sense a growing heaviness inside.

On the penultimate day there is an earthquake, a minor tremor. Everything shakes and for a spilt-second afterwards there is a hum as the shelves settle and people whisper their surprise. He looks right at me then and we don't need books to say anything more.

~~The end is nigh~~.

And then it is here: the last day. I arrive to see him frantically working, surrounded by a flurry of notes. Leaves of A4 fall from the edge of his table and creep across the floor towards me in a pale tide. I stalk the shelves slowly, leadenly, without purpose. My fingers linger over Graham Greene, *The End of the Affair*. I can't do it. Later, in the afternoon, when just

three hours remain

he gets up and comes back with *The Salt Road* by Jane Johnson. It's his most cryptic choice yet. I spend the remainder of the day racking my brain and Googling reviews. Was it a reference to tears? Was he saying he was going to be sad without me? It was so hard to decipher. Or was it intentionally meaningless, symbolic of our imminent separation? I pack up and leave first, miserable and frustrated.

Doomed.

A week later I am buying a coffee in a coffee shop I swore I'd never go in but there is nowhere else to go. As I step back out onto the street I read the sandwich board outside the newsagents next door. ONE MILLION BOOKS TO BE SENT DOWN THE MINES. I buy a paper and juggle my coffee to turn the pages and find the rest of the story. It turns out that the books from the library have a strange, beautiful fate: they're going to be stored in salt mines the size of seven hundred football pitches, deep beneath the Cheshire plains. The perfect environment, experts say. Whoever knew there were so many in there, or so much room under Cheshire. I will have to remember to catalogue this final revelation when I find somewhere to sit.

And then I look up from the paper and see that he is making his way down the street towards the coffee shop I thought neither of us would ever go into. He walks faster outside than he did in the library and I'm surprised but also not surprised to see him and I find I don't move out of the way, I just stand there between the sandwich board and the doorway and when he gets close he has to almost stop still. He smiles a fresh smile in the solid September light. I move to one side and then back, to the other side and then back. It takes me all my courage to say something – to speak to him in words that aren't static and flat on their backs. I hear my voice come out into the air and the sound of it shocks us both.

'How did you know about this?'

I stand there on the pavement, shaking the paper, my coffee hot in my hands, my face cracking with expectancy.

ROBERT SHEARMAN

The Dark Space in the House in the House in the Garden at the Centre of the World

I.

Let's get something straight, right from the outset, okay? I'm not angry with you. Mistakes were made on both sides. Mistakes, ha, arguably, I made just as many mistakes as you. Well, not quite as many, ha, but I accept I'm at least partly to blame. Okay? No, really, okay? Come on, take those looks off your faces. I'm *never* going to be angry with you. I promise. I have wasted so much of my life on anger. There are entire aeons full of it, I'm not even kidding. And it does nothing. It achieves nothing. Anger, it's a crock of shit.

Isn't it a beautiful day? One of my best. The sun's warm, but not too warm, you can feel it stroking at your skin, it's all over your bare bodies and *so* comforting, but without it causing any of that irritating sweaty stuff under the armpits. Though I do maintain that sweat's a useful thing. Look at the garden. Breathe it in. Tell me, be honest, how do you think it's coming on? See what I've done, I've been pruning the roses, training the clematis, I've been cutting back the privet hedges. Not bad. And just you wait until spring, the daffodils will be out by then, lovely.

No. Seriously. Relax. Relax, right now! I'm serious.

The apples were a mistake. Your mistake, my mistake, who's counting? My mistake was to set you a law without explaining why the law was being enforced, that's not a sound basis for any legal system. Of course you're going to rebel, right. And *your* mistake, that was eating a fruit in which I had chosen to house cancer. Well, I had to put it somewhere. You may have wondered about all those skin sores and why you've been coughing up blood and phlegm. Now you know. But don't worry, I'll fix it, see, you're cured. Poppa looks after you. As for the apples, good source of vitamin A, low in calories, you just wait til you puree them up and top them with sugar, oh *God*, do I love a good apple crumble. I'm not even kidding! Keep the apple with my blessing. As for the cancers, well, I'll just stick them in something else, don't worry, you'll never find them.

Give me a smile. We're all friends. Smile for me. Wider than that.

And so, are we good? Cindy, and what is it, Steve. I think we're good. The fruit is all yours to eat. The air is all yours to breathe, the flowers are all yours to smell. The beasts of the world, yours to name and pet and hunt and skin and fuck. We're good, but there is one last thing. Not a law, ha ha, I wouldn't call it a *law*, ha ha, no, okay, no, it's a law. Don't go into the forest. The forest that's at the heart of the garden, the garden at the centre of the world. The forest where the trees are so tall that they scratch the heavens, so dense that they drown out the light, where even the birds that settle on the branches come out stained with black. What, why, because I said so. What? Oh. Yes, fair point. Because at the centre of the forest there stands a house, and the house is old, and the house is haunted.

Okay.

Okay. I'll be off then. Night, night, sleep tight. Don't let the bedbugs bite.

⁂

So they went into the forest the very next morning, man and wife, hand in hand, and they dropped apple cores along the way so they could find a path back again. 'Like Hansel and Gretel!' said Cindy, because God had told them all his favourite fairy tales when they'd just been children, he'd tucked them up tight in beds of leaves and moss with stories of enchanted castles and giant killers and heroes no bigger than your thumb; 'you can be Gretel,' agreed Steve, 'and I'll be Hansel!' And the trees were so tall and so dense and so black, and they were glad they were doing the thing together, it made them both feel warm and loved. And they didn't know for how long they walked, it may have been days, and they worried they might soon run out of apple cores, but presently they came across the house, right there at the forest's heart. And it was a magical house, a structure of red brick and thin chimneys and big bay windows and vinyl sided guttering. It didn't look very haunted; 'it's probably quite nice inside,' said Cindy, and Steve agreed, but he held on to her hand tightly, and both hands began to sweat. They went up to the front door, and peered their way through the panel of frosted glass, but they couldn't see anyone, nothing inside was moving. Steve rang the doorbell, and Cindy called 'Hello!' through the letterbox, but there was no answer, and they were both about to give up, turn about, pick up their apple cores and go home, when the door swung open anyway at their touch. It didn't creak, the hinges were too good on that door.

Cindy and Steve wondered if they could squeeze themselves into something as small as that house, they'd been so used to the sheer size of the garden that was their world. And they exchanged glances. And they shrugged. And they went in.

In the kitchen there were two places set for dinner, and at each place there was a bowl of porridge. 'Like Goldilocks!' said Cindy, because God really hadn't stinted himself in his fairy tale telling; 'you can be Goldilocks,' said Steve, 'I'll be the bear!' They ate the porridge. They both privately wondered who the porridge belonged to. They both wondered if the porridge belonged to the ghosts. They thought they should go home, but it had started to rain. So they decided there was no harm in staying a little longer; they inspected the sitting room, the bathroom, a nice space under the stairs that could be used for storage; 'Hello,' Cindy called out, 'we're your new neighbours!' And they looked for the ghosts, but saw neither hide nor hair of a single one. The rain was coming down hard now, it was a wall of wet, and it hit the ground fierce like arrows and it was so dark outside you couldn't see where the rain might have fallen from, how it could have found its way through so dense a crush of treetops. And the apple cores were gone, maybe they hadn't been dropped clearly enough, maybe the birds had eaten them, maybe they had long ago just rotted and turned to mush. So they had no choice, they had to stay the night together in a haunted house, maybe they could find their way back to their own garden in the morning, maybe.

The bedroom was big. There were two large wardrobes, and there was a dressing table with a nice mirror to sit in front of and do make-up, and there was a huge bed laden high with blankets and pillows. Cindy and Steve got under the covers.

They both listened out for the ghosts in the dark.

'I'm frightened,' said Cindy, and reached out for Steve's hand. And Steve didn't say he was frightened too, that his stomach felt strange stuffed as it was with porridge, that his skin felt strange, too: tingly and so very sensitive with a mattress underneath it and sheets on top of it and this smooth naked body lying next to it, brushing against it, tickling its hairs, yes oh yes. 'Don't be frightened,' said Steve, 'I'll protect you, my Snow White, my Rapunzel, my unnamed princess from Princess-and-the-Frog,' and he kissed her, and they had never kissed before, and they explored each other's mouths much as they had explored the house, with false bravado, and growing confidence, and some unspoken sense of dread. They pushed their tongues deep into each other's dark spaces. And slept at last. And dreamed of ghosts. And of what ghosts could even possibly be.

II.

So this is where you are! I couldn't find you! I didn't know where you could be, I thought maybe you were in the maze. You know, that maze I made for you, with all those tall hedges, cylindrical archways, and any number of delightful red herrings. The maze, yeah? I thought, they're playing in the maze, it's easy to get lost in the maze, what a hoot! So I waited for you at the exit, I thought you'd come out eventually, I'd surprise you by saying boo! And I waited quite a long time, and one day I thought to myself, you know what, I don't think they're in this maze at all. The maze I made for them. So where could they be?

I felt a bit of a prawn, I must say, waiting outside a maze for six months all primed to say boo. Getting the exact facial expression right. I got a bit bored. I made a lot more cancers and viruses to keep my mind occupied. Oh, and I made the antelope extinct. Hope it wasn't a favourite.

But, no, you've found the house! And good for you. Oh, did I say that you shouldn't come to the house? Did I? Doesn't sound like me, hang on, trying to think, no. No, I can't imagine why I would have said that. You want a house, with what, rooms and floorboards and curtains and shit, then you go for it. Much better than a maze. Really, *fuck* the maze. I want to hear you say it. Say it with me. Fuck the maze. *Fuck* the maze. That's it, so you can see, I've no problem with the maze at all. I'm not even kidding! You have whatever you like, I never want to hold you guys back, I love you, I'm crazy about you. You have your house, a house with a roof to keep the rain off.

(In fact, sorry about the rain. Not quite sure what that's about. Very frustrating, must be leaking somewhere up there, the sky's cracked, got to be. And yeah, I can hold the rain back, but the thought of that crack, at that poor cowboy workmanship, it makes me a bit cross, quite *angry*, and when I get angry, it seems to rain all the more, and you know what? It's a vicious circle.)

And you've found the wardrobes! Picking through the cupboards as if they're yours, and they *are* yours, of course they are. Look at you, Cindy, no, I mean, *look* at you. All those dresses, all those shoes. That skirt, ha, that doesn't leave a lot to the imagination, ha, that really emphasises your, um, ha, hips, ha ha! And make-up too. Though? If I can? Make a suggestion? The lipstick. Goes on the lips. Hence the name, yeah. . . . And you, erm, Steve, you look nice too.

No, not *all* the house is haunted. Did I give you? That impression? No, the kitchen's fine. The bedroom's fine.

The sitting room, fine. Bathroom, ha, there are no bogey-men lurking behind the toilet cistern. No, it's the attic. It's the attic that has all the ghosts in. You haven't found the attic yet? You didn't know there even *was* an attic? Well, there is. I wouldn't go looking for it, though. No good will come of it. Sometimes you stand underneath that attic, at the right spot, you can feel the temperature drop, there'll be a cold chill pricking over your skin. There'll be a sickness in your throat, your heart will start to beat uncomfortably fast. Listen hard enough, press your ears up to the ceiling, you can hear *whispers*. The whispers of the dead. No, I wouldn't bother, you just stick with your mercifully spook-free lavatory, you'll be fine.

Is that the time? I should go. It's a long way back to the garden, and it's getting late. No, how kind, shouldn't stay for dinner, maybe next time. But how kind. What a kind thought. How lovely. I'll get back to my maze, my silly little maze, that'd be best. Better hurry, it's pissing down out there.

Night night then. You be happy. Be happy, and stay happy. You both mean the world to me. Night night, sleep tight. Don't let the bedbugs bite.

It took them four days to find the attic. It was difficult. No matter whereabouts they stood they felt no chill or nausea, and their heartbeats remained frustratingly constant. Eventually it took Cindy balanced upon Steve's finer shoulders, reaching up and prodding at the ceiling – a painstaking operation, and one that took a lot of straining and swaying – before Cindy said that beneath the wallpaper she felt something give. They cut away the wallpaper with a kitchen knife. They exposed a hatchway — small, neat, perfectly unassuming.

It hadn't been opened in a long time. No matter how much Cindy pushed at it it just wouldn't move; Steve at last had to help, crouching down with Cindy on his shoulders and then springing up tall, sending his wife fast up in the air and using her as a battering ram.

The rather dazed Cindy poked her head through, and Steve called up, 'Can you see anything? Can you hear anything?' Cindy remembered the fairy tales she'd been told, Jack climbing his way up a beanstalk to dangers unknown, Aladdin lowered into the darkness whilst his uncle stayed safe up top. 'No, nothing,' she said. Steve got up on to a table and climbed through the hatchway after her. There were a few nondescript boxes piled up, mostly cardboard; they contained years-old fashion magazines, clothes, toys, a stamp collection, stuff. If there was a chill, it was only because they were away from the central heating. If there was a whispering, it was just the lapping from inside the water tank, or the sound of wind playing against the roof.

And if they were disappointed, neither Cindy nor Steve said they were. They went back to their ordinary lives. Cindy learned how to use the kitchen, she'd make them both dinner from tins she found in the cupboard. Steve found a DIY kit, and would enjoy banging nails into things pointlessly with his hammer.

And in bed they continued to explore each other's bodies. Steve discovered that Cindy enjoyed it when he nibbled on her breasts, but that he should stop well short of making the blood thing leak out; for her part, Cindy quickly learned that sucking at appendages rather than biting down hard and chewing was always a more popular option. They examined and prodded at each and every one of their orifices, and into them would experiment inserting opposing body parts; they found out that no matter what they tried to stick up there, be it tongue, finger or penis, the nostrils weren't worth the effort. And soon too they realised that it was better to do all of these things in the dark, where the ridiculous contortions of facial expressions on their spouse's face wouldn't put them off.

They listened out for the ghosts. They never heard them.

One night Steve woke from his sleep to find Cindy wasn't there. He put on his favourite silk dressing gown from the wardrobe, went to look for her. At last he found her in the attic, sitting on the floor, rocking back and forth as she cried so hard. At his approach she started, turned about, looked at him with startled teary eyes. 'Where are our ghosts?' she begged to know. 'Where's the chill, the sickness in my stomach? I can't feel anything. Why can't I feel anything at all?'

III.

You were thinking of a nursery, right? The attic for a nursery, that was the plan?

Oh, sorry, didn't mean to make you jump! Coming round unannounced, very rude, but I tried the doorbell, and there was no answer, and I thought, shall I just pop in anyway, why not, good friends like us don't need to stand on ceremony. I can see why you didn't hear me. You're pretty busy. Pretty . . . entwined, there.

Don't stop on my account. I can wait. You finish off, I don't mind, I'll watch. Oh. Oh. Suit yourselves.

Speaking of which! I can see that you've discovered the joys of sex. Which is nice. I'm a little surprised, ha, by your choice of *partners*, I mean, doesn't it strike you as a bit incestuous? You crazy kids, what will you get up to next! I don't mind. I don't mind at all. I mean, it makes me wonder why I invented the zebu in the first place, you don't fancy the zebu, all those dewlaps? It could have been a baby zebu that's growing inside your stomach this very moment, imagine what *that* would have looked like!

Oh, you didn't realise? Yeah, you're pregnant. Congratulations! Some men don't like women when they're pregnant, but Cindy, I must say, you look *great*, all shiny and hormonal like that, all your body parts swelling every which way. And yeah, well done too, Steve, yeah. And you're going to need a nursery. Which is why, I'm sure, you had only the best intentions when you ignored my *advice* and went up into the attic. And why not, good choice. Babies are great, but take it from me, they're annoying, they cry a lot, there's a lot of noise and sick, keeping the baby up in the attic out of earshot is a good plan. Clear away the boxes, there'll be room up there for all those baby things babies seem to like. It's all just junk, there's nothing in there to worry about.

Except, of course, for that *one* box. The one with the padlock on. Now, you two and I have had a bit of a laugh, haven't we? It's all been fun. But this time I'm really telling you. It's a padlock. That's a big fucking hint. You are not to open the box. You are not to open the box. I forbid it. I absolutely forbid it, and yes it's a law, it's an order, it's a commandment from up high. Leave the box alone. No matter what you hear inside. No matter what the ghosts inside the box say to you.

Lightening the mood! – any ideas for a name for the baby yet? No? Well, I'm just saying. You want to name it after me, you can. Call it God, or Lord, or Jehovah, or some such, and I'd be honoured.

The daffodils are out. They look beautiful.

Well, I can see you have things to do. Some of which

will no doubt make you drowsy, you'll be wanting to sleep soon. So, you know. Night night. Sleep tight. Don't let the bedbugs bite. No, I really mean it, I'm not sure, but I think I put cancer in a few of them, the bedbugs are riddled with cancer. You see a bedbug, you *run*.

So they smashed the padlock, and straightaway they heard them, the whispers inside – and there were so many, there was so much chatter, the conversations were all over-lapping so they couldn't make out what was being said! 'Open the box!' said Cindy, too eagerly, and 'I'm trying!' Steve snapped back, and it seemed such a fragile little box, but now the lid was heavy, they pulled together and the lid raised an inch, and husband and wife had to prise their fingers painfully into the little gap to stop it from shutting again. And the whispers seemed so loud now, how could they not have heard the ghosts before? And they both felt a bit ashamed of that. Ashamed that they'd been carrying on with their lives quite pleasantly, cooking and ham-mering and shagging away, and had never paid the ghosts any attention. Cindy looked at Steve, and smiled at him, and thought, *I wonder if I'll find someone new to talk to.* And Steve looked at Cindy, smiled back, thought, *I wonder if their orifices will be prettier.* Because they both loved each other, they knew they did; but how can you tell what that love is worth if you're nothing to compare it to?

They took strength from each other's smiles; they heaved again; the box opened.

The whispering stopped, startled.

Inside there was a house. Not a proper house, of course, but a doll's house. And it wasn't *quite* like their house; it too had red bricks, and thin chimneys, it had windows and guttering, but they could see that the sitting room was smaller, there was less wardrobe space in the bedroom, the toilet had a broken flush.

There was no one to be seen.

'Talk to us!' said Cindy. 'Come back!' said Steve.

They wondered if they could squeeze themselves into something as small as that house. And they exchanged glances. And they shrugged. And they went in.

IV.

God didn't talk to them for a long while after that.

❧

There was lots of fun to be had in the haunted doll's house.

Their new neighbours were very kind. Their names were Bruce and Kate. Bruce and Kate knocked on the door one day, said they'd heard people had moved in next door, wanted to welcome them, hoped they'd be very happy. They invited them round to dinner. Cindy and Steve didn't know what to bring, but they found a bottle of old red wine in the back of one of the kitchen cupboards, and Bruce and Kate smiled nicely at it and said it was one of their favourite tipples. Kate made a really lovely casserole, 'nothing fancy, just thrown it together,' and Bruce laughed and said Kate's casserole was a secret recipe, and it was certainly better than anything Cindy could have come up with. Bruce was in charge of dessert. Bruce and Kate showed Cindy and Steve around their modest house, and it wasn't much different to Cindy and Steve's, only in the bathroom their flush *did* work, Cindy and Steve felt a little bit jealous. And Bruce and Kate had a seven-year-old daughter called Adriana who was quite pretty and very polite and did ballet and whose drawings from school were hung on display for all to see with fridge magnets. 'Can see you're expecting!' said Kate to Cindy, and Cindy agreed she was; Kate said it'd be nice for Adriana to have a new friend to play with, maybe. Bruce and Kate were dead. They were dead, but they didn't seem to know they were dead. Cindy and Steve could see right inside them and there was nothing but ash in there and their souls were spent. They smelled of death, their eyes rolled dead in their heads, they waddled awkwardly as they walked. Adriana was dead, and when at Kate's indulgent prompting she agreed to show the new neighbours a few choice ballet steps it was like watching a broken puppet splaying cack-legged across the floor. 'Well done!' said Kate, and clapped her dead hands, and Bruce laughed the most cheery of death rattles, and Cindy and Steve were good guests and clapped and laughed too.

Bruce asked Steve what he did for a living, and Steve said that he was between jobs. And Bruce was very kind, he got Steve an interview at the bank where he worked. And Steve spent the day sorting money and counting money and giving money to people through a little glass grille. He'd never seen money before, but he liked the feel of it, and in return for his hard work he was given money of his very own. Steve determined he would try hard to collect an awful lot of it. And the bank manager was very nice, and congratulated Steve on his efforts, and gave him a promotion, which basically meant that Steve gave more money to different people through a slightly bigger glass grille. And the bank manager was dead, and the customers were dead, and Bruce was still dead, of course, Bruce being dead wasn't going to change in a hurry. And Steve would sometimes after work go out with Bruce to a pub and get pissed.

And Cindy wanted to work at the bank too, but Kate told her she'd really be better off staying at home and looking after her baby. And Cindy could feel it kicking inside, and decided it was high time she let the baby out, she couldn't be sure but she thought it had been kicking inside there now for *years*. She went to the hospital and the doctors were dead and the nurses were dead and all the patients were dead, and some of the dead patients were so ill that during their stay at the hospital they died again and somehow got even *deader*, that was so weird. And a particularly dead nurse told Cindy she had to push the baby out, and that she was being very brave, and that they were having this baby together, and *push*. And out came the baby, and the baby was crying, and still kicking away, and the nurse cooed and said it was a beautiful little girl, and Cindy felt a sudden strange rush of love for her child, a stronger love than she'd ever known before, stronger than anything she'd felt for Steve or, even, God; but the baby was dead, it was dead, Cindy was given it to hold and it rolled its dead eyes at her and burbled and sneezed and Cindy could see there was no soul to it, just ash. 'I don't want it,' she said to the dead nurse, 'I don't want this dead baby,' and she thought of how this ashen soulless corpse monster had been feeding inside her stomach and she felt sick. The dead nurse told her again the girl was beautiful, she was such a *beautiful girl*; 'You keep it then,' said Cindy. But apparently that just wasn't an option, and Cindy had to take the stillborn little parasite home and feed it and pet it and read it fairy tales and give some sort of shit when it screamed.

And Steve didn't like their new baby daughter either – he *said* he did, and he played with it, and sat it on his knee, and asked after it when he came back home pissed from the pub – he didn't say *anything* against the baby at all, come to think of it; but Cindy knew he must hate it, because she hated it, and they were one flesh, weren't they, they were soulmates, they were *one*. And they still had sex, it was a little more routine than before, even a bit desultory – but Cindy didn't mind, she wasn't quite sure what part of the sex process had resulted in this baby growing inside her in the first place; she thought that if they did the sex thing very quietly, almost without passion, almost as if they weren't really there at all, then they wouldn't draw attention to themselves. Then no future daughter would see.

Cindy stayed at home. Cindy felt trapped. Cindy remembered the fairy tales she'd been fed when she was a child. Damsels with long hair locked away in high towers, princesses forced down to sleep on peas. Mothers pressed into bargains with grumpy evil dwarves who wanted to steal their first-born. Cindy didn't meet many dwarves, no matter how hard she looked – not at the supermarket, not at the kindergarten, not at the young mothers' yoga group that the erstwhile Kate had persuaded her to join. Cindy knew that the dwarves wouldn't have been much use anyway, the dwarves too would have been dead.

'I love you,' Steve would say to Cindy, each night as they got into bed, and he meant it.

'I love you,' Cindy would say back, and she meant it too.

Steve had met someone at work, a little cashier assistant less than half his age. He didn't expect her to like his whitening beard and his receding hairline and his now protruding gut. She fucked him at the office Christmas party, and he told her it had to be a one-off, but she fucked him three more times in January, and an astonishing fifteen times in February, she was really picking up speed. 'Tell me you love me,' she'd say afterwards as she smoked a fag, ash in her ash, and he'd say he did, and he thought that maybe that was even true, just a little bit; she'd wrap her corpse legs around him and her dead matted bush would tickle the bulge of his stomach, and then he was inside her, he was inside something that felt warm and smooth but he knew was really so so cold and was rotting away into clumps of meat. He thought her death would infect him, he hoped it would. He wished he had the sort of relationship with Cindy where he could talk about his new girlfriend, who bit by bit was becoming the very centre of his world, the little chink of garden at the heart of his day. But Cindy had never been one to share things with, nothing of any importance. And some nights he'd cry.

Once in a while they'd try to escape the doll's house. But they couldn't find the exit. They took their dead daughter on a holiday to Tenerife, but there was no exit there, not even as far away as Tenerife. When their dead daughter was older, and wanted holidays of her own, with disreputable-looking dead boys who had strange piercings and smelled of drugs, Cindy and Steve took their very first holiday alone. They went to Venice. They drank wine underneath the Rialto. They were serenaded on a gondola. They made love in their budget hotel, and it felt like love too. It felt like something they could hold on to. And sometimes, back at home, when Steve cried at night, or during the day when Cindy stared silently at the wall, they might think of Venice, and the memory made them happy.

This account focuses too much upon the negatives, maybe. They had a good time in the haunted doll's house, and the ghosts were very chatty, and some of them were kind.

v.

'Hello, hello!' Beaming smiles all round. 'Well, here we are! Here we all are again!' A clap on the host's back, hearty and masculine, a kiss on the hostess's cheek just a little too close to the mouth. 'So good to see you both, I'm not even kidding! I brought some wine, where would you like it?'

They showed him the house. He made appreciative noises at the sitting room, the kitchen, the bedroom. He admired the toilet, Steve pointed out to him the flush, and how he'd fixed it with all the DIY he'd learned. They settled down at the kitchen table and ate Cindy's casserole, and they all agreed it was really good.

'Well. Well! Here we all are again.'

God was wearing a sports jacket that was meant to look jaunty, but it was two sizes too big for him; God looked old and too thin; the jacket was depressing, it made him look diminished somehow. The wine he'd brought was cheap but potent. The conversation was awkward at first, a series of polite remarks, desperate pauses, too-big smiles and eyes looking downward. The wine helped. They began to relax.

Cindy asked if they could return to the garden.

'Go backwards?' said God. 'I don't know if you can go *backwards*. You crazy kids, what will you think of next!'

They laughed, and shared anecdotes of mazes and apples, of fairy tales told long ago.

God mused. 'I think the idea is. If I think about it? I think, the older you get, and the more experienced you get. And the more you realise how big the world is, and how many opportunities are in front of you. Then the smaller the world becomes. It gets smaller and smaller, narrowing in on you, until all that's left are the confines of a wooden box.' He coughed. 'You could say that it's a consequence of maturity, of finding your place in the world and accepting it, of discovering humility and in that humility discovering yourself. Or, maybe. Ha. It's just a fucking bad design flaw. Ha! Sorry.'

He drank more wine, he farted, they all laughed, oh, the simple comedy of it all.

'But,' God said, 'this world isn't all there is. It can't be. There must be a way out. At the very centre of the world, there's a dark space. Don't go to it. Don't go. It isn't a law. I'm not, ha, forbidding you. But I think,' God said, and his voice dropped to a whisper, and he looked so scared, 'I think there are ghosts there. I think the dark space is haunted.'

'Well,' said Steve, eventually. 'It's getting late.'

'It *is* getting late,' said Cindy.

'No doubt you'll be wanting to get back home,' said Steve. 'Back to your garden and whatnot.'

'Back,' said Cindy, 'to your maze.' She took away God's wine glass, put it into the sink with a clatter.

God looked sad.

'I'm dying,' he said.

'Oh dear,' said Steve.

'That's a shame,' said Cindy.

'I've been mucking about with too many cancers. I've got nobbled by the ebola virus, I've come down with a spot of mad cow disease. It's all the same to me. I've been careless. Too careless, and about things that were too important.' He coughed again, gently wiped at his mouth with a handkerchief, looked at the contents of the handkerchief with frank curiosity. He blinked.

'Shame,' said Cindy again.

'And I wanted to see you. I wanted to be with you, because we're family, aren't we, you were always my favourites, weren't you, you're my favourites, did you know that? I'm crazy about you crazy kids. I miss you. I miss you like crazy. We never had a cross word. Others before you, others after, well. I admit, I got angry, plagues, locusts, fat greasy scorchmarks burned into the lawns of the Garden of Eden. But I love you guys. I love you, Cindy, with your big smile and your deep eyes and your fine hair and your huge norks and your sweet sweet smelling clit. And you, what was it, Steve, with your, um. Winning personality. If I have to die, I want to die with you.'

His eyes were wet, and they couldn't tell if he were crying or rheumy.

'This world can't be all there is,' he breathed. 'It can't be. I have faith. There *must* be a way out.' He opened his spindly arms wide. Give me a hug.'

So they did.

'Because,' said God. 'You loved me once. You loved me once, didn't you? You loved me once. You loved me. Tell me you loved me. Tell me you loved me once. You loved me. You loved me. You loved me.'

They buried their father in the back garden that night. It wasn't a grand garden, but it was loved, and Cindy and Steve had planted flowers there, and it was good enough.

Then they went indoors, and they began looking for the dark space at the centre of the world. They'd been to Tenerife and to Venice, they'd seen no dark spaces there. So they looked in the kitchen, they cleared out the pots and the pans from the cupboard. They looked in the bathroom behind the cistern. They looked in the attic.

They decided to go to bed. It had been a long day. And Steve offered Cindy his hand, and she took it, a little surprised; he hadn't offered her a hand in years. They both liked the feel of that hand holding thing, it made them seem warm and loved. They climbed the stairs together.

They looked for the dark space in the bedroom too, but it was nowhere to be found.

They got undressed. They kicked off their clothes, left them where they fell upon the floor, stood amidst them. They came together, naked as the day they were born. They explored each other's bodies, and it was like the first time, now there were no expectations, nothing defensive, nothing to prove. He licked at her body, she nuzzled into his. Like the first time, in innocence.

She found his dark space first. It was like a mole, it was on his thigh. He found her dark space in the shadow of her overhanging left breast.

She put her ear to his thigh. Then he pressed his ear against her tit. Yes, there were such whispers to be heard! And they marvelled that they'd never heard them before.

She slid her fingertips into his dark space, and they numbed not unpleasantly. He kissed at hers, and he felt his tongue thicken, his tongue grew, all his mouth was a tongue. They both poked a bit further inside.

They wondered if they could squeeze themselves into something that was so small. They looked at each other for encouragement, but their faces were too hard to read. They wondered if they could dare. And then she smiled, and at that *he* smiled. And they knew they could be brave again, just one last time. They pushed onwards and inwards. And they went to someplace new.

STUART EVERS

What's in Swindon?

T HE LAST TIME I'd seen Angela Fulton she was leaving Wigan's World Famous Winter Wonderland dragging a three-foot stuffed rabbit through a field of dirty fake snow. I'd won the luckless animal for her moments earlier, but it had not proved the conciliatory gesture I'd hoped. Instead, Angela had stormed off in exasperation and hurled the rabbit onto a pile of rubbish sacks by the exit. I watched her leave and in an impotent rage headed to the refreshment tent and got drunk on mulled wine. By the time I got home, all of her possessions were gone.

We were in our early twenties then, the two of us pale and skinny and living in an exacting proximity to each other. We knew no one else in Wigan, and made no effort to mix with people outside of our respective jobs. Instead we sat in our smoky one-room flat, talking, occasionally fighting and in the evenings making love. Afterwards, by the light of a low wattage bulb, we'd inspect our bodies: the constellations of bruises our bones had made.

How we endured such isolation for so long is hard to say. I suspect now that we found it somehow romantic to live such a shabby, closed-off life. We had no television, no phone; just our books and an inherited Roberts radio that only picked up Radio 4 and John Peel. There was the odd excursion to Liverpool and Manchester, to the Lakes and the Wirral, but for the most part we stayed indoors, paralysed by the intimacy of our affair.

Of course, it could not last, and those last few months were unbearable, horrible. Without either of us noticing it, the real world slowly began to encroach. I started to go out on my own and come back late at night, drunk and insensible. Angela would disappear for hours without ever divulging where she was going. To spite her, one evening I came home with a second-hand television set and placed it pride of place on the dresser. In retaliation, Angela insulted the way I looked, the length of my hair, the state of my clothes, the number of cigarettes that I smoked, my childish sense of humour. One night she threw a book at my head and called me a thoughtless fucking cunt. The next morning neither of us could remember what I was supposed to have done.

Angela was not my first love, nor I hers; but it felt like we should have been. Years later, I would imagine her laughing at the appearance of my new girlfriend; in idle moments wonder whether she still dressed the same way. Late at night I'd remember her naked body, picturing her with a waxed bikini line that she'd never had. In such moments, I would consider trying to find her again, but didn't have a clue where to begin. Still, the compulsion was there: like a seam of coal, buried yet waiting to be mined.

That morning I left my house and took the Underground to work, bought a coffee and drank it at my desk while reading the newspaper. At 9 a.m. there was the usual departmental meeting, which was swiftly followed by a conference call. I ate my lunch in the courtyard and then

33

browsed in a bookshop. When I arrived back in the office I had nineteen voicemails: three of which were just the sound of a phone being replaced on its cradle.

I answered the emails, returned the phone messages and was about to make my afternoon cup of tea when the phone rang again. It was a number I didn't recognise. I hesitated, then picked up the receiver. There was a pause and then a woman's voice asked for Marty. She was the only one who'd ever called me Marty.

Angela sounded exactly as she had before, and I recalled for a moment the way she used to breathe heavily in my ear. She asked me how I was and I stuttered, then stood up for no good reason. There was a pause, a long one. Eventually, I asked her how she'd got my number.

'You're on the Internet,' she said.

'I'm on the Internet?' I said.

'Everyone's on the Internet,' she said.

I asked her what she wanted. She asked if I was with someone. I said no, not really. She told me she'd booked us a hotel. I asked where. She said Swindon.

'What's in Swindon?' I said.

'I will be.'

'I'm not sure,' I said. 'I mean —'

'Oh come on,' Angela said, 'we both know you're going to say yes, so why waste the time?'

I had never been to Swindon before, and all things considered, it is unlikely I will ever go to Swindon again. On the train, there was something about the look on the passengers' faces, a certain kind of blankness. I burrowed into my seat and took out a newspaper, but realised I'd read it all at breakfast. Instead I went to the buffet car and came back with some Chinese nuts and a can of Bass. In the silent carriage, I apologetically opened the can and crunched the snacks. I tried the crossword, but couldn't concentrate on even the simplest clue.

We arrived and in the midst of a stream of impatient commuters, I made my way out of the station. The line for the taxis was long and I waited behind a couple recently reunited by the 17:04 from Cardiff. The woman had her hand in the man's back pocket, and he was kissing her. Even in Swindon, I thought, train station kisses are the most romantic of all.

Eventually I got a cab, and the driver tried to engage me in conversation – something about bus lanes – but I ignored him and looked out the window, hugging my overnight bag to my chest. Swindon looked like a business park that had got out of hand. There was an eerie, almost American sadness to it; the entertainment parks, the shopping malls, the parades of smoked glass office blocks, their windows reflecting the dying sun. The hotel was at the intersection of several arterial roads, a squat building cowering against the flow of traffic.

The hotel lobby was shockingly bright, decorated with plasticky blonde wood. The receptionist – a young man with ginger stubble – was sullen and gittish. I told him there was a reservation in the name of Fulton and he puffed out his cheeks.

'Yes, that's correct, sir. However, the reservation appears to be for a Ms Fulton, sir. And we require the person named on the reservation to be present before any party can take possession of their room or rooms,' he said.

'Did Angela not put my name down as well?'

'Evidently not,' the receptionist said and waving his hand answered the ringing telephone.

I stood there not knowing exactly what to do. 'I'm

so sorry,' the receptionist said into the receiver, 'would you mind holding for one moment, madam?' He turned to me.

'Sir, why don't you wait for your friend in the bar?' he said, pointing to some double doors. I picked up my holdall and followed his outstretched arm.

The bar was just as plasticky and woody, and just as garishly lit. There was a drunken party of young women sitting around a huge round table and three Japanese businessmen silently drinking Stella Artois. I ordered a gin and tonic. It felt like the right kind of drink to be seen with by an ex-lover – from a distance it could easily be sparkling water. The barman was sullen and gittish. He tried to get me to order some olives. I ordered some olives.

Angela arrived soon after. She looked older, but in a good way. Her hair was kinky and her eyes fizzed like Coca-Cola. She stood at the bar and drank the remainder of my gin and tonic.

'Say nothing,' she said and took me by the hand.

The bedroom was brown and cream and functional. She sparkled in her silver dress and pushed me against the wall. For a moment we were twenty again. She guided us both back to a time when we didn't need to worry about interest rates and love handles, pensions and cancer, stunted ambitions and broken dreams. I made sure that she came first; I could have done it with my eyes closed.

After we were finished, she looked at me expectantly and rolled over. I held her tightly and she leaned herself back into me. She smelled of sex and shampoo; her breasts heavier in my hands.

'Hello,' she said, 'I've missed you.'

'Me too –'

She interrupted me with a long, sloppy kiss, which she then abruptly curtailed. She put her hands on my chest and then on my face, like she was piecing me together from scrap.

'But . . . no, this is all wrong,' she said. 'Something's not right. I feel . . .' she shivered. 'I can't explain it.' Angela bent down and kissed me again, experimentally.

'You smell . . . I don't know, wrong,' she said, sniffing my skin.

'What, like bad?'

No. Just not like you. She looked puzzled for a moment then glanced at the bedside table.

'Did you quit smoking?' she said, like it was an accusation.

I laughed. 'About five years ago now.'

'Quit? I never thought you'd quit. Not ever.'

I didn't like the maddened look in her eyes: she was naked, but not in a good way.

'Well I did.'

I put my hand to her hip and she looked at me as though I had deceived her.

'Do you still drive that Vauxhall Viva?' she said.

'It was a Hillman. And that's long gone. You don't need a car in London.'

She pulled up the bedsheets and put her head in her hands.

'I never should have done this,' she said, 'it was a terrible, terrible idea.' She turned her back on me then and made her way to the en suite bathroom. She had cellulite on her thighs. It was sexy in a way that women just don't understand.

'I don't get it,' I said to the closed door. 'You spent the whole time we were together bitching about how much

I smoked and how bad it was for me and how much it stank, and now . . .' She opened the door wearing a white towel. The shower was running.

'Look, Marty,' she said, picking up her abandoned clothes. 'I wasn't going to say anything, but the truth is that I'm getting married.' She smiled, tiredly. 'Or at least I was thinking about getting married. But then out of nowhere, I started thinking about you. About those years we had. And what I have with Declan, well it's not like that. Nothing could be like that. So I had to see. I couldn't let it just go. Couldn't let it just disappear into nothing. I hoped that, you know, that it would all just slot back into place, but . . .'

'But what?'

'Look at us,' she said. 'We're not children any more. In my head, you're this romantic, childish, impossible boy with all these impossible dreams. But that's not you. Not any more. And I can't bring him back. And even if I could, could you really live like that again?'

'Yes,' I said. 'Yes I could. And if that's all it is, I could start again. I could start right now!'

'You know there's more to it than that.'

She laughed and closed the bathroom door. As the water fell I imagined her getting married, the flowers in her hair and the string ensemble playing as she walked down the aisle. Her husband a lunk of a man; his head shaved and looking like a security guard in his hired suit and tails.

When she came back into the room, Angela was fully dressed, her hair wet at the ends. She picked up her overnight bag.

'I'm sorry, Marty, I just needed to know,' she said and kissed me lightly on the cheek.

She shut the door behind her and I went to the window

to see her drive away. Across the bypass, a twenty-four-hour supermarket glowed red and blue. I pulled on my jeans and headed out to get supplies.

Alice in Time & Space and Various Major Cities

ALICE WAS DRESSED as Susan Sontag and heavily bruised over one eye.

'The sybian machine malfunctioned,' she explained.

We high-fived each other five times. Having not met since the very earliest days of the 21st century, during a time of considerably higher interest rates, many things had changed since our last encounter. Historically we had entered a new era of super volcanoes and climate chaos, the American psyche was in turmoil, and a fraud of frankly massive magnitude had spread its tentacles around the globe. Alice, meanwhile, had maximised her previous feminine assets with a fine new hairstyle and some thick, horn-rimmed spectacles.

'Save me from the water!' she cried above the hubbub.

Amidst the foggy ardour of cats and cigarettes, an evening of typical British rubbishness was in progress: about forty people as pink as cherry blossom dancing awkwardly, quaffing semi-precious beers. The music was upbeat, modern; the smell of damp urinal rather disheartening.

'What water?' I mouthed.

'The metaphorical waves,' she spluttered, employing jazz hands.

I grabbed her by the shirt sleeve and pulled her in the direction of relative safety . . .

'. . . so, how are you?' I asked (strolling through the green municipal places of the city along beautiful boulevards between gilded gateways across courtly courtyards beneath towering watchtowers down a sticky marble ramp glistening with recently dispelled nightclub semen).

'Life could not be better,' Alice beamed.

'Oh,' I said. 'I am sorry to hear that.'

Soon we came to a nameless neon-lit place vibrating to the sound of Blink 182 and the Klaxons. Among empty chairs and empty tables we drank freshly ground Latin American coffee and spoke of this and that, as was our custom.

'Thank you for saving me,' she added. 'Even though I wasn't in any danger.'

'It was nothing,' I told her.

'I know,' she agreed.

Alice had developed a keen morphine addiction and now wore a cap set a little off her face so her features weren't cast in too much shadow. Her outlook, however, remained affably morose.

'And what are you doing at the moment?' I interjected into the silence.

'Nothing,' she remarked. 'I'm remarkably Buddhist in that respect.'

She lit an imaginary cigarette and I watched in silence as the light skipped illogically across her face, lucent as porcelain, moustachioed veins softly broken like the compromised promises of certain former newspaper proprietors: 'It's actually been a rather unusual period in my life.

In order just to survive I withdrew into myself – but I fell backwards into a thesis rather than a living/breathing recognisable narrative. And I fell much further than I initially intended: swimming down along the gutter of Time, through the intestines of the past, into the colon of yesteryear where I found it easier to love landscapes rather than actual people. Life was kind of defunct for a while and I was faced with a fearful dilemma. Quietly seated in a moment of clarity and rare abstinence, I realised I was the victim of a conspiracy that nobody understood except me,' she explained. 'Anyway, we all of us now live in extraordinary times. The old days have fallen into disrepute. The old ways are redundant. Nobody knows what the hell is happening any more . . .'

I pondered her oblique words and ordered an extra large Jack Daniels.

'I agree,' I agreed. 'But I wonder,' I wondered, 'if this strange meeting of ours might not be more than just mere chance. I mean, unexpected things do happen – all the time – for a variety of hugely improbable metaphysical reasons nobody actually understands. So perhaps you and I being here, together, like this, is part of some totally unfathomable higher plan . . .'

'No,' she declared confidently. 'I don't think so. There are no happy endings anymore. *As for the rest of our lives?* Well, absolution lies ahead. *Somewhere.* I'm almost certain of it . . .'

Alice abruptly swelled up her chest to nearly twice its regular dimensions.

'LET'S TALK ABOUT YOU,' she roared and told me more about herself: the single spies she had known, the disappointing doctors she had dated, the obscure acting dynasties she had partially infiltrated, the disastrous sexual escapade that had finally driven her to New York and back again. ('Thought it was love. Turns out it wasn't,' she summarised.)

The room shook with nervous erotic tension.

'Alice!' I boomed at her bust. 'I am not here merely to trade quips. I had adjusted my psyche to the possibility that I might never see you again. But I have indeed thought of you often during all these years you've been painstakingly avoiding me. With love, affection, occasional erections. You are a truly lovely woman with a face entirely your own. The type of face any heterosexual man might conceivably die for – if such unlikely circumstances ever arose. You are as graceful as Grace Kelly, as baleful as Christian Bale, as capable as Capability Brown – though not quite as angry as Kenneth Anger.'

Suddenly stern and Edwardian, Alice ruptured my rapture.

'*Sheeesh*,' she sheeeshed. 'Be warned. I have formed some strong romantic attachments of late. My latest is Sam Squeeze, the part-time megalomaniac. He's a philanthropic philanderer and rapes the planet for profit – but I like him.'

Her eyes seethed with the same cool azure blue most commonly associated with Californian swimming pools.

'A man could get lost in those eyes,' I swooned.

'Many have tried,' she admitted. 'Few have returned.'

Thirty-five shots of rum later Alice was bubbling horribly through the nose; a fine example of traditional British phlegm. As one of the few remaining upright among all the horizontals, I transported her on my back through the foul-smelling city until we happened upon the streaming yellow lights of a grimy fortress oddly reminiscent of a chic, slightly effeminate hotel.

'What is this strange, indefatigable place?' I asked.

'My new apartment,' she gurgled.

In the foyer a wealthy young couple were having a self-consciously hip discussion about Feyerabend's epistemological anarchism by the archaic lifts while a continual flow of barely conscious people continually passed by: venerated Beatniks, bohemian painters, delinquent poets, Jamaican punks, acidic Jewish wives, elderly transvestite rockers, overweight sex addicts in leopardskin trilby hats . . .

Alice cuffed my wrists with her hands.

'Sense the sentient transience?' she gushed. *'The clamour of dying glamour?* No shame or vacuum cleaners here. Only porn shoots and cocaine parties in the corridors. This place is vivid and otherworldly, filled with magical possibilities, seasick creatures, rock 'n' roll ghosts, dead luminaries. Ryan Adams lives here in a permanent bordello atmosphere alongside other famously alienated people like Vigo Mortensen, Donald Rumsfeld, Irving Berlin, Salvador Dali, Phil Silvers, Baron von Munchausen and Condoleezza Rice . . .'

Just then a green-eyed queen swished past pursued at some speed by a hugely flustered Henri Cartier-Bresson.

Her room was lit by one small red light bulb, like a Korean brothel. Alice lay down naked on the chaise longue and began arousing herself with *The Giant Book of Russian Erotica*. 'I am deflated in places I oughtn't to be deflated,' she confessed, indenting her cheekbones for dramatic effect. 'Why persist with a life that makes no viable sense?'

'I don't know,' I admitted, adopting an effusively Gallic stance. 'I've been short of major epiphanies myself lately.'

Alice groaned and reclined with some cocaine and a very modern novel.

'I like your tits, Alice,' I informed her. 'Both of them. They erect my penis in a fairly surprising manner.'

Her labia quivered visibly.

'Thank you!' Alice ejaculated. 'But I've been much vexed of late with the greater questions of the cosmos. *What is Time? What happens to us when we die? Why do we dream? How did we get here? Where are we going next? What is the shape of space? Has Darwin killed God? Did God kill Darwin? Why can't the free market provide adequate protection against unexpected catastrophes? What makes a Superpower super? Is flying really the safest way to travel? When did the Arts become so dull? Why do Spaniards lisp? Who was Kurt Weill? Why is fashion in spring different to fashion in winter? Why aren't thin people fat? What's the secret of the perfect soufflé? If Heidegger had the answer, what was the question? Can Capitalism be good for you? Is everything we know about the universe actually wrong?* So you see I now have a scholarly commitment to the doomed predicament of all humans in this universe: Death, God, the afterlife, Fate, every aspect of our mutual sense of inescapable humanity. Often I am lost in short-term elations, abortive dreams, floating in the sewage of discarded daydreams. Yet the struggle to achieve some kind of resolution is potentially pointless. Dissatisfaction often comes when a long-strived for ideal is attained and the reality realised. Thus there is no hatred in my heart. No blood beneath my fingernails. Just let us celebrate, a little nostalgically perhaps, the end of love – although that point is unlikely to be officially reached until everybody on the planet is legally dead . . .'

I entered her shortly afterwards with Chekhovian precision.

One week later. An urgent electronic transmission from Alice arriving urgently:

It's time for extreme measures! Like a wistful 19th Century heroine intent on seeing something of the rest of the world, I need to get out of this festering shit-hole. Fast. (You know, before it's too late.) There are too many cunts in this city and they've got me all boxed in. I can't hole up here anymore. They're gonna hunt me down. Unless I leave now they're gonna nail me. I've been visiting too many restaurants of late. It's a grim, culinary existence and from now on I plan to eschew food entirely. I'm leaving tomorrow btw. But I shall return. One day. Maybes le hiver. xxxx[1]

Gradually the climate changed around me.

First came floods, then the smell of rotten eggs. An age of perpetual Coldplay descended, overshadowing nearly everything with the ambience of Brian Eno. Epic days ensued during which even hardcore bachelors circumnavigated the planet submerged by global gloom and widespread pandemonium. Ballet was declared illegal, latent homosexuality mutated into a more virile form and hypothyroidism became particularly rife within the theatrical community. Men still walked and talked as they had in times of David Foster Wallace, but the city I once loved was now illegally occupied by a vague gastronomic expansion of more than a thousand nouvelle restaurants. As the world slipped inexorably toward mindless idolatry, I sat down Indian-style and did nothing, unintentionally alienating several friends and numerous acquaintances. Time, meanwhile, was still in motion. Summer turned to winter, quite quickly, before anybody noticed. Soon it was June in January. Next it was bitterly cold and rather autumn. I waited alone inside my four blazing walls like a sad typist whose dreams of a career with promotion

1. The news prompted me to take off my clothes and spray myself all over with Happiness, the healing fragrance for emasculated men. Then I stood proudly in front of the mirror for about a month, studying myself in near-gynaecological detail.

prospects had never quite materialised. I slumbered, dear reader, oh how I slumbered. With just a very fake sense of American optimism to keep me going I retired to bed with a bottle of Benzedrine and read Garcia Marquez's *One Hundred Years of Solitude*, Flann O'Brien's *At Swim-Two-Birds* and *The Third Policeman*, Isaac Babel's *Collected Short Stories*, Borges' *Labyrinths and Other Inquisitions*, Thomas Bernhard's *Correction*, Rudy Wurlitzer's *Nog*, Isaac B Singer's *Gimpel the Fool*, Bernard Malamud's *The Assistant and The Magic Barrel*, Ralph Ellison's *Invisible Man*, Malcolm Lowry's *Under the Volcano*, everything I could find by Samuel Beckett, Knut Hamsun's *Hunger*, Max Frisch's *I'm Not Stiller* and *Man in the Holocene*, Dinesen's *Seven Gothic Tales*, Tommaso Landolfi's *Gogol's Wife*, Thomas Pynchon's *V*, John Hawkes's *The Lime Twig and The Blood Oranges*, Grace Paley's *Little Disturbances and Enormous Changes at the Last Minute*, Susan Sontag's *I, Etc* and *Against Interpretation*, Tillie Olsen's *Tell Me a Riddle*, Campbell's *Hero with a Thousand Faces*, Bellow's *Henderson The Rain King*, Updike's *The Coup* and *Rabbit, Run*, *The Paris Review* interviews, Rust Hills' *How We Live*, Joe David Bellamy's *Superfiction*, the Puschart Prize Anthologies, Sternburg's *The Writer on Her Work*, André Breton's *Manifestoes of Surrealism*, Robert Motherwell's *Documents of Modern Art*, Hugh Kenner's *A Homemade World*, Flaubert's *Letters*, Mamet's *Sexual Perversity in Chicago*, Joy Williams' *The Changeling*, Joe David Bellamy's *The New Fiction*, Tim O'Brien's *Going After Cacciato*, Amos Tutola's *The Palm-Wine Drunkard*, Ann Tyler's *Searching for Caleb*, Kenneth Koch's *Thank You*, Frank O'Hara's *Collected Poems*, John Ashbery's *Rivers and Mountains*, Wesley Brown's *Tragic Magic*, Roland Barthes' *Mythologies and The Pleasure of the Text*, Robbe-Grillet's *For a New Novel*, Ann Beattie's *Falling in Place*, William Gass' *In the Heart of the*

Heart of the Country, Fiction and the Figures of Life and *The World Within the Word*, Mailer's *Advertisements for Myself*, Anthony Burgess' *A Clockwork Orange*, Celine's *Journey to the End of the Night*, Kobo Abe's *The Box Man*, Italo Calvino's *Invisible Cities*, Peter Handke's *A Sorrow Beyond Dreams* and *Kaspar and Other Plays*, André Breton's *Nadja*, John Barth's *Chimera*, Walker Percy's *The Moviegoer*, Jayne Anne Phillips' *Black Tickets*, Peter Taylor's *Collected Stories*, Colette's *The Pure and the Impure*, Carver's *Will You Please be Quiet, Please*, Leonard Michaels' *I Would Have Saved Them If I Could*, Max Apple's *The Oranging of America*, Cheever's *Collected Stories*, Eudora Welty's *Collected Stories*, Flannery O'Connor's *Collected Stories*, Ishmael Reed's *Mumbo Jumbo*, Toni Morrison's *Song of Solomon*, Carlos Fuentes' *The Death of Artemio Cruz*, Milan Kundera's *The Book of Laughter and Forgetting* and Wayne C Booth's The *Rhetoric of Fiction*, the second edition with the additional afterword and supplementary bibliographical information. *Word of Alice* only reached me when I ran into her best friend Judith in the Velvet Quarter eating Japanese noodles in a bloodstained wedding dress with Jimmy the Monkey. It was late September or mid October or early November; Time was in a state of flux and decay and I was wearing a bowler hat and carrying a tightly-rolled umbrella tucked under one arm.

'How are things?' Judith asked.

She looked me over with splendidly serious eyes. Now easing into her thirties she was at her zenith of loveliness despite having taken over 40,000 Ecstasy tablets in the past three years.

'Oh,' I explained, 'you know.'

(In truth, there was little I wanted to share about the past flat drab years, though I bigged up my time in the

Victorian psychiatric hospital where I had been admitted under Section 4 of the Mental Health Act, 1983.)

' – and *Alice . . .*' I added, fairly warily. 'What about Alice?'

Judith arched an artful eyebrow . . . Alice (it transpired) was now penniless in Asheville, NC, specialising in over-romanticised tales of murder and psychosis, and had just turned herself into a kind of novel – a very short novel she called

ALICE IN TIME & SPACE
AND VARIOUS MAJOR CITIES
A Very Short Novel

How I long for earthy Northern contact, Alice thought to herself. But all things considered, would it be better to suck the thin, pristine penis of Albert or have a blazing afternoon orgasm with Roger or perhaps have my bottom licked scrupulously clean by Richard?

'Alice!' Bloom cried, in some mental distress. 'Alice!'

'Bloom, you damned fool!' Alice shrieked wildly. 'Capitalism is dead! God is dead! Religion is dead! Ideology is dead! Romance is dead! Love is dead! The author is dead! The novel is dead! The reader is dead! Basically everybody's got it coming to them sooner rather than later.'

(From Chapter 36: 'Alice in the Land of Avarice and Abstentionism')

– thus novelised, Alice was a paradoxical apparition, an appendix, a secondhand bible, a bowdlerised bibliography, a quixotic creation, a creature of the early hours, a shimmering chimera, a criminal compendium of wilfully bad intentions and completely random lifestyle decisions: sweeping across the surface of the globe – travelling among unknown men – visiting Athens, Ankara, Andorra, Algiers, Amsterdam, Addis Ababa, Adelaide, Atlanta, Austin, Antwerp, Acapulco, Anchorage, Atomic City, Albuquerque and various other alliterative places in order to elicit their maximum poetical effect. Though by novel's end she had returned to her apartment and begun typing up her experiences, Alice (the girl who broke through the staunchest defences and made sense of traditionally nonsensical things) was lost to me now, drifting toward an unintelligible world, misplaced somewhere in the space-time continuum, each of us spinning in our own separate orbits, wholly engulfed by the vastly impressive size and scale of the rest of the post-Aristotelian universe . . .

THE END

The Visit

I T H A D B E E N a day of weather; snow and wind, sunshine and rain. Water dripped from the overhanging hedges in the drive and the path was thick with pine needles. Brendan made a mental note to sweep them up once Pat had gone. He stopped before the gates and pulled his trousers up by their creases to check his shoes and thought that maybe he should've worn his boots. He walked on. Pat would make him forget. Pat could make you forget all kinds of silly woes. He glanced over at Coogan's and noticed the stars and stripes flag, still and wet on the pole.

After McCaughey's he looked over at Joy Callan's neat line of laundry crowning her raised side lawn: a small satin-rimmed blanket, black stockings, two blue ballroom gowns, a pair of orange nylon pillowcases. As he approached her house he saw her in the yard, bright and chic in pink slacks and a tight white jumper. She was raking up leaves. He watched her part the dresses then yank the wet leaves into a pile. It made him smile; she might have hung the gowns out after she'd raked, but Joy always seemed to do things differently to others. And anyway, he was glad, because she made the task so mesmerising. He recalled how after her husband had gone she had kept body and soul together by moonlighting, rather originally he thought, as a mushroom picker in Clones. Otherwise, as a relief teacher she had taught both his children in the Friary, though she had not been popular. He waved and wondered would she be at the Square tomorrow. He made a mental note to call in one of these evenings with the picture of Sean's wedding in the paper.

Walking on, his thoughts returned to Pat. He looked forward to seeing him. There would be much talk of the 'great adventures' as Brendan called them, the London times, the days of the Black Lion where he had been manager for nearly a decade and where Pat had been its most notorious barfly. He was proud to think he'd organised some of London's most celebrated lock-ins, booked musicians from Dublin and Doolin and Donegal, and had the likes of David Bailey and Donovan in attendance. Soon he and Pat would be reminiscing about those times, about the dog races at Hackney and White City, the times they'd played poker in Holland Park with Jack Doyle.

He walked up the cobbled lane towards the station. He could see clearly on the cold day the sprawl of the town towards the hills. The trees by the church were draped in ropes of white lights, and a flurry of flags hung from Carroll's Apartments. He was amazed to think that here, in this small dot on the face of the globe, he and Pat would stand together tomorrow evening and see the President of America.

The big station clock said ten to three. He had a few minutes yet to gather his thoughts, stare over at the glass wall of the brewery. He sat outside on the iron seat. The gulls hovered above him, filling the air with their cries. The sweet wort's more pungent today, he thought, as his gaze fixed on the huge copper kettle glistening through the glass. It had been his first job in the brewery to wash the kettle out once the sweet wort had been siphoned off. He would then prepare it for the following morning's shipment of hops and grain. He had spent the best part of five years inside that copper drum, up to his ankles in the remnants of fresh hops, proteins and sticky clumps of caramelised sugar. It had given him time to think; to put into perspective all that had happened in '74.

There was a rumble on the tracks. He turned and saw the sleek green body of the Express stack up like a metallic snake along platform two. He walked over and watched from the ticket office. The doors of the carriages swung open. Women with pull-up trolleys, young men in dishevelled suits, Mrs Little and her daughter, Edel. As the crowds dispersed he saw a ghost; the tall, hulking frame of Pat Coleman standing stock-still on the busy platform. The springy hair was all white, the once firm chest now visibly lax. Brendan watched his friend remove a cigarette from behind his ear, ask a girl for a light, then take three or four concentrated puffs before flicking the stub behind him onto the tracks. Pat's short-sleeved shirt seemed frowsy and unironed; the thick brown arms with their blue tattoos recalled to Brendan Pat's nickname on the sites: Popeye. Popeye Pat had had the strength of ten men, and once, in a drunken rage, Brendan had seen him flatten as many.

He followed Pat's gaze. Up to the pale, elusive sky of the North; out to the striking sweep of the white-capped hills, the green spire of the Protestant church peeping up against them. He began to feel unfamiliar pangs of pride for the town, as if through Pat's languorous impression, he, too, was glimpsing it for the first time. The town was his wife's town, and he had always found it hard to appreciate its people with their wariness, their industrious, practical approach to things. His wife had been right, he *had* put up a resistance. She had accused him often of hiding away in the brewery kettle like a genie. But the friend-ships he had formed here had been without the closeness of his London bonds. The men he knew from the town were nothing like that famous man on platform two.

He watched Pat follow the exiting crowds up the wooden ramp. He'd forgotten about Pat's hip. The two of them would seem a right pair with their battered bodies, their war wounds, struggling up the road to the house. They'd have to get a taxi.

At first Pat walked right past him, then doubled back, grabbed his hand with a warm, heavy shake and twirled him round in the air, both feet dangling. The familiar horseplay made Brendan feel warm and young inside. He suggested they take a taxi but Pat said he wanted to walk.

'What d'you think?' Brendan said, turning onto the prosperous-looking road.

'Looks good,' Pat replied in his reedy voice, the rapid Limerick lilt fully intact.

'You know you're to stay as long as you like.'

'Well, I'll see. It'd be something to hear Clinton. After that, I've a whole load to see in Kilkenny and Limerick.'

Pat's sallow tight face spoke of his abstinence. No beads of sweat across the brow or lip, no dank odour. Gone were the umber circles and the frantic eyes. *If you don't stop drinking you'll die*, Brendan had said quietly into Pat's ear on his last visit to Guy's. Pat had often said it was those words together with his friend's insistence he *could* quit that had saved his life.

Past the Texaco garage, Pat stopped to watch Nick O'Hare sort through a trailer of wicker goods. 'That's Nick,' said Brendan. 'Used to be a coach with the town's football team, now runs a type of yoga place in that house.' Pat seemed enthralled by Nick's wares. There were fusions of weave and dried flowers, shopping baskets with long handles, knee-high linen boxes stained in a dark cinnabar, as well as a small Lloyd Loom-style chair. Bowls of felt sunflowers, papier-mâché apples and grapes littered the tarmac drive. Pat went up to the brass sign on the pillar and mouthed the words engraved on it: *Vipassana Centre*.

'How are ya?' Pat shouted over to Nick, who was down on his hunkers editing strands of grass from the baskets.

'Well, Brendan,' Nick replied, thinking it had been Brendan who had hollered. 'I'm making these for the President. I'll bring one up to you.'

'Do,' Brendan replied, waving, and carried on hurriedly, hoping Pat would take the hint and move on with him.

'D'you ever go in there?' Pat asked.

'Jesus, no.' Brendan replied.

'I'd love one of those baskets for Fidelma.'

'Haven't I a dozen in the garage?' Brendan said.

Walking on, he tried to turn the conversation towards London and the Black Lion. He asked Pat if he'd heard anything from the old gang, from Mocky Joe in particular. Mocky Joe's success at cards had enabled him to live in London for over a decade without working. One night, weeks before Brendan had left London, the flame-haired Mocky Joe had been picked up under the Prevention of Terrorism Act and held. Of all the men he and Pat had known that had been stopped under the Sus laws or questioned under the PTA, Mocky Joe was the only one the police had ever charged. He'd served twelve years. At first Pat seemed to have no recollection of him, but eventually put a face to the nickname. 'The poor fucker,' Pat said, 'I went to see him and he didn't know me at all.' Then Brendan thought of the time of his own arrest, the long night of questioning in Harrow Road police station, and of the lie he had told there.

Pat stopped to look over the bridge. 'The kids used to walk all the way along that one time, trying to catch frogs,' Brendan said, realising he had never himself walked the banks of the narrow river. The sedge rustled below where they looked and an ochre-coloured frog leaped out, springing from one clump to the next along the shallow rim of the water. He saw that Pat was bewitched by the frog, its golden skin pulsating like a loud gold watch; it seemed alien, larger than the small green specimens the kids had once brought from the banks. They watched the bright interloper go on with the river, thinning out towards Toberona and Castletown. Though it seemed hard for him to get the memories out of Pat, Brendan looked forward to the chats they were yet to have about all the great adventures.

Closer to home, Pat wanted to stop off at Cheever's. Brendan reluctantly followed Pat into the store, which was festooned on the outside with green and white bunting. A flag with 'Welcome Bill' stencilled on it protruded from the wall.

'That's a bitter day, Brendan,' Mrs Cheever said as she sorted through the newspapers. Brendan nodded then guided Pat towards the freezer at the back of the shop.

'But you have it lovely and warm in here, missus,' Pat shouted over to the stout woman. Brendan saw Mrs Cheever look up at them and move a fallen strand of hair away from her face, her fingers black with print.

'I'm with him. Over from London for the visit,' Pat said.

'Very pleased to meet you,' Mrs Cheever replied, in her singsong voice. She walked over and put a copy of *The Democrat* under Brendan's arm.

'Here. The son's wedding is in that. Have another for safe-keeping.'

Pat picked out a pack of Galtee cheese, some rashers, a half-pound of lard, a sliced white batch-loaf, a copy of *Ireland's Own* and Kimberly biscuits. In the basket they looked like something from a 1950s tourist brochure, the type of provisions Brendan himself had bought years ago in Mandy's in Willesden when he was homesick.

'Pat, you're my guest. You're to spend nothing.'

'Always pay my way, you know that,' Pat insisted.

By Callan's Brendan heard harp music and stopped. It sounded loud and sad. He saw Joy seated at the table, stiffly staring into a hand-mirror. He saw her catch sight of him, then Pat, who was examining her winter flowers. He wanted to call out but she dashed from the room. He sensed they had stumbled upon a private moment, a low. His pace quickened. When he stopped he heard Pat laughing behind him.

'Now there's a woman in need of cheering up.'

'Can't tell you the times I've wanted to call in to her but never do.'

'You have to get yourself a reason, man.'

'She likes dancing, I drag my left leg. All I can think of is bringing things, flowers maybe.'

'All good, but it's not a reason. Ask her to come to Clinton with us.'

It had not even occurred to him to ask Joy Callan to go to the Square with them. One evening in Cheever's he had spoken to her about the President's visit and had been impressed by her enthusiasm, by her belief that the visit would act as some kind of salve for what the town had been through in the last three decades.

This is it, Brendan said, opening the turquoise gates to the house. Pat gasped at the long, shrub-filled lawns.

Brendan watched his friend hobble back to the gates, rest his hands on his hips and look up and down the bunting-covered road. Blue cigarette smoke swirled around Pat's head like a halo.

'How in the name of God do you manage?' Pat said, retreating towards him.

'I have a home-help. Her husband comes up, does the lawn in summer.'

'Good job you have such friends and neighbours.'

Brendan stopped. Surely Pat had seen how preoccupied and standoffish the people here were, and how different he was from them. Surely Pat had observed this.

'The people of this town never liked me, Pat. Nor me them. There's been no friends for me like the London ones,' Brendan said.

'Could have fooled me,' Pat replied, darting towards the woody fuchsia hedge. He broke a piece off, smelled the tiny buds. Shepherding him into the house, Brendan put Pat's assessment of his neighbours and friends aside. After all, what did Pat know?

Later, Pat suggested they bring their tea out onto the porch. Brendan followed Pat out with the teapot and an ashtray. The mauve dusk had begun to blacken. Small birds thronged in the elder bushes. Occasionally, passers-by saw them from the glow of the street-lamp and waved. He was determined to get Pat talking.

'Do you not remember all that carry on in Maida Vale in '74?' he said at length. Pat shook his head, hurled the end of his tea into the grass.

'You don't remember the police bulldozing into me, asking me about you?'

'No.'

'Came ramstaming into our digs in the middle of the night, said they wanted to question me. Took me to

Harrow Road station, said someone the spit of you killed an off-duty soldier in Maida Vale. I said – well, ya know what I said. That you were with me up in White City.'

'I don't remember much of that time at all, Brendan, tell ya the truth.'

Pat seemed uneasy. Perhaps he should not have brought the incident up, but all evening Pat's memory had been hazy. He'd wanted to jolt Pat into remembering. Especially since the lie he had told had cost him so much: a precipitous move from London to this hardnosed border town, a move he hadn't wanted to make, had regretted all the years since.

He brought the cups inside. From the kitchen he could see Pat glaring meditatively out into the greeny-black of the garden, his hands cupped. It had been impossible to draw him back to the days of the Black Lion. Pat had just wanted to look out into the night and talk about the barely discernable shrubs: the mahonias, hebes, winter sweet. Surely this white-haired man with his apparent amnesia and love of plants was not the same Pat. Popeye Pat, who'd had the strength of a bear and may or may not have killed a man in a nightclub in Maida Vale. It dawned on Brendan then, that it had all changed, his London: the lads, the infamous Black Lion lock-ins, the dramas with the PTA. At nine, Pat said he was ready for bed, that abstinence had made a lark out of him.

At around five Brendan thought he heard Pat stir. When he got up, the blinds had been raised, the curtains pulled. December glowed in the empty kitchen. He saw a folded note and a crisp twenty Euro bill under a cup on the table. He picked up the note. Pat's heavy spidery scrawl had almost punctured the page. He scanned it quickly. Something about Pat heading off to see his wife's people in Kilkenny, and that he would call in again next week. The note continued: *Once you said I'd die if I didn't stop drinking. You said you knew I could do it. You saw the best in me and it gave me hope to go on. Now, for god's sake man, would you ever give that town a chance. And give my regards to Bill and Hillary.*

Brendan opened the door to the backyard. The smell of sweet wort filled the room. He realised how familiar that smell was, how he'd smelled it daily now for almost twenty-five years. Perhaps, whilst he wasn't looking, he had entered the tapestry of this place after all. Trembling, he picked up the phone to ask Joy Callan if she would walk with him later to the Market Square to see the President.

Half-mown Lawn

ANNIE IS READY for an empty house by the time everyone has finally gone home. She spends the first hour or so flitting from room to room, straightening cushions and rescuing the odd missed wine glass from the bookshelves upstairs, before ending up in her rocking chair staring out the bedroom window as frail white clouds sidle past.

Below, the long grass of the half-mown lawn shivers in the wind, the mower still stood at the checkpoint between the cut and uncut. Where the grass is short, blades poke from the soil like a crew cut. The shape pressed into the long grass calls for her attention but she refuses its demands.

At the kitchen table, Annie tears a piece of paper from a message pad. She writes the name of the local store at the top. Underneath she writes headings: Frozen, Fresh, Dairy, Fruit/Veg, Household. Underneath each she creates columns of her needs, organising oven-chips, apples, sponge scourers and skimmed milk into manageable groups. Under the heading Fresh she writes whole chicken. The words hold her for a moment before she crosses them through with a single line and writes chicken breast in the space beneath.

She stands in the pantry, waiting for the empty spaces on the shelves to reveal what is missing from her list. The gaps between the pickle jars, rows of cereal boxes and tinned goods are indecipherable, redacted text that she cannot make sense of. Back at the table she turns over her paper and makes another list. On it she writes,

Things I will miss:
Him polishing his shoes every morning
The way he looked in a suit
His mixing five different types of cereal for breakfast
The quiet knock of his briefcase on the hall floor
The sound of his breath, warm on my back at four in the morning

She continues like this until long past the local shop's closing time, resigns herself to driving to the all-night Tesco.

In the aisles, Annie searches for the items on her list, filling her trolley with washing-up liquid, onions, bread and those biscuits he liked. As each item drops into the trolley, she crosses a list entry out with an Ikea pencil found in her coat pocket. She flips the list to check the back and finds herself staring at the things she will miss. Her eyes flick up at the signs hanging from the false ceiling of the supermarket, as if simply by looking she will find the section he is hiding in.

At the checkout she places her shopping on the conveyor, slotting a customer divider directly behind her things. Her items move slowly toward the till and she rearranges them, grouping together the fruit and vegetables, the dairy, the household goods. The checkout girl swipes the shopping through in a flurry of bleeps and Annie struggles to keep pace as she fills up her bags for life.

'£57.81,' says the checkout girl.

Annie rummages in her handbag.

'I seem to have left my purse at home,' she says.

The checkout girl huffs then hits the button next to the till to call a supervisor.

'It's my first day. I don't know what to do about this,' she says.

'I don't know what to do either,' Annie says, her eyes checking the aisle signs once more.

Annie takes two eggs, a slice of ham, the cheese and the last of the tomatoes from the fridge. The oil warming in her small omelette pan, she cracks the eggs into a cup and scrambles the yolks with a fork. The ham and tomato sit in chopped piles beside a mound of grated cheddar.

The puddle of oil spreads across the frying pan, seeking the heat, and she waits until it is ready before pouring out the eggs. She sprinkles ham, then tomato, then cheese, letting each sink into the surface of the egg before adding the next. Once finished, she deposits the omelette onto a clean plate, leaving the pan and chopping board beside the cooling hob.

On the table a single space is laid and she empties the remains of a bottle of red into her wine glass. She takes her time with the meal, slicing small mouthfuls from the omelette, her wine sitting untouched beside her plate. In this way she avoids the kitchen window.

Paul, Jenny and the grandkids stayed behind after friends and family had gone home. Jenny busied herself, stacking the glasses and plates into the dishwasher.

'I could mow the lawn for you, Mum,' Paul said.

'Don't you fucking touch it,' Annie heard herself scream.

A beat of silence followed before the children whispered 'Granny did a swear' and Jenny ushered them into the kitchen for ice cream. Flushed, Annie collapsed into an armchair but didn't cry.

'It's okay, Mum,' Paul told her. But it wasn't.

Now, Annie picks up the phone and dials his number.

'Mum?' he says. 'Is everything okay? Do you need me to come over?'

'Can you mow the lawn tomorrow?' is all she says.

'Of course. You're sure?'

She presses the end call button without replying.

Annie removes the dirty dishes from the dish washer and places them in order upon the work surface, before turning on both taps. The sink fills quickly and she takes each item from the pile and scrubs them in the soapy water. The caked-on stains of the Pyrex dishes take time and elbow grease to remove. Twice she empties the sink replacing the brown greasy water with fresh suds.

The draining board is soon crammed and she pulls a clean tea towel from the drawer. Each item is dried and tucked away in the kitchen cupboards, one at a time, even the cutlery, before she refills the sink a third time and sets about the final pile of dirty crockery. Only now, with the garden growing indistinct in the dusk, does Annie look out through the kitchen window at the dimming outline of the shape in the grass, her hands continuing to scrub at food stains already removed.

Annie shuts off the lights in the front room and takes her book and a cup of jasmine tea upstairs. She sits in the rocking chair, her book on her lap and lets her tea grow cold. When, finally, she looks down at the shape in the grass it is barely visible in the dim light provided by the nearby street lamps.

Only days ago, though it already feels much longer, she sat in the rocker by the window, reading, as he started the job. She had smiled, glancing down at him mowing the lawn, before losing herself in her book. It was the sound of the mower shutting off, too soon for him to have finished, that pulled her from her reading. When he turned to look up at the window she saw it in his face. He crumpled onto the lawn as she rose from her chair.

Annie flosses, careful to run the white thread deep below the gum line where plaque forms, just as the hygienist showed her. She brushes her teeth for the full two minutes. In the mirror her mouth fills with toothpaste foam until she has to spit. A quick cold-water rinse then she switches off the en-suite light and closes the door behind her.

Their double bed has fresh sheets; probably Jenny being helpful. Annie climbs in her side of the bed, lies facing where he should be. There is no indentation or crease in the bottom sheet or pillow on his side, any trace of him smoothed out when the sheets were replaced. She scoots over and buries her face in his pillow but it is the smell of detergent that fills her nostrils.

Unable to sleep, Annie pulls her dressing gown about her, walks downstairs, slips on her garden shoes and steps slowly out, taking care only to walk on the mown part of the lawn. The summer night air is warm even for the time of year. Where he fell, the shape of him remains pressed in the long grass.

Annie crouches and runs her finger around his outline, the compacted grass inside like a crop circle in the shape of a man. She strokes where his cheek pressed to the ground, almost sees his face bristling with irritation as it did the morning she complained about the unmown lawn.

Without looking around, she climbs into the outline of him and lays down, careful to keep herself entirely within its boundaries. She gently places her head on his broad chest, spooning her legs onto his, just as she used to when they were younger. The smell of cut grass is an embrace now, where, in the hospital, kissing the fingers of his cooling hands, it had overwhelmed her. Annie lies still and listens for his heartbeat.

'I'm the Guy Who Wrote *The Wild Bunch*'

Veteran Hollywood screenwriter Brady Donovan died a year ago this week. The Irish novelist Julian Gough interviewed him a few months before his death. They talked about Donovan's time working with Sam Peckinpah, during Peckinpah's ill-fated first attempt to film The Wild Bunch *in 1965. The following account is edited together from several conversations.*

YEAH, I'M THE guy who wrote the original script for *The Wild Bunch*. That was a tough job. Sam wasn't well at the time, he'd started drinking heavily on his previous shoot, and he was coughing up things that looked like frogs. I hadn't worked with him before, but I'd worked with guys who had, so I knew what to expect. We met out at his ranch, sat on the porch. He offered me a bottle of some kind of Mexican beer. You see them in New York now, with a slice of lime stuck down the neck of the bottle, cost you five bucks, like some kind of fashion thing. But the Mexicans, they just ran that lime round the top of the bottle to disinfect it, threw it away. Rats, you know, in the cellars. You can get that disease where your eyeballs go red and your skin turns yellow. And in Mexico in those days, there was no point washing anything. The water was more dangerous than the dirt. So anyway, I said no thank you, Mr Peckinpah, I never drink while I'm writing. He laughed and drank them both himself. He had a refrigerator out on the porch, so he didn't have to leave his chair to get a beer. So we wrote that script together, for *The Wild Bunch*, on the porch, him drinking Corona, me drinking some water I brought in a bottle.

So what's this film about, Mr Peckinpah, I asked him. It's about a bunch of killers, hiding out in the hills in Mexico, he says. And I don't want them prettied up, mind. They ain't got a sensitive side and they ain't misunderstood. But they will die together rather than lose their balls, you understand? When they're given an easy way out at the end, when they could walk away at the cost of giving up their friends, they shrug and they spit at the ground and they say no thank you.

So we wrote that film, and I think it was a good script. Sam seemed happy, and he took it to United Artists, but they were having money troubles around then, and they said Sam, we like it, but we ain't in a position to do it, and they passed. And I think he was a little hurt by that. So he took it back to Warner Brothers, which he didn't like to do because he'd just had a bad experience with them on *Major Dundee*. They'd taken it off him and butchered it. But Warners said yes, perfect, just do one more draft. The usual one-two.

Because we did another draft, and the notes started to come back, and they weren't good. The producers were getting cold feet, because this film was maybe the first honest Western, these guys weren't the Gary Cooper type of cowboy. I mean, even for Peckinpah, this was a pretty brutal movie. His thing was, no redeeming features.

Don't blame anything on their fucking childhoods, these guys are just, you know, they like killing. So anyway, the studio say, it's great, but there's no love interest. We won't get the young couples in, if it's just a bunch of guys. And Sam is saying, it's called *The Wild Bunch*! It's about a bunch of guys! And they say yeah, but just give us a love angle and we can sell the fuck out of this motherfucker. No love angle, says Sam. Well, then, just give us a woman we can put on the poster, for Christ's sakes. This argument went on for days, Sam just saying no love angle. Eventually they say, no love angle, fine, make her a nun. But, you know, a sexy nun. And Sam, he's tired, he's drinking, it's been days of this, he says OK. So I write in a sexy nun.

And I think that was where the script started to go wrong. Because she, you know, she stood out somewhat in this script, we had to rewrite a bunch of scenes to find her something to do, and she stood out among all these guys, there was a lot of conflict between her and the guys in the script. And conflict is sexy, you know, conflict is drama, so as soon as she was in there, it changed the whole script. And pretty soon the notes came back, yeah, we like the nun, give her more scenes. But Sam is tearing his hair out, he's saying, you know, how wild are these guys if a fucking nun is telling them what to do? So he was, you know, maybe they can rape and kill her. And the suits were, uh, maybe not. I suggested, how about we make her a little older, older than these guys and more experienced, so that it makes some kind of sense that she can order them around. But the suits had signed up this young English actress who was hot at the time for the part of the nun, so we compromised, and made the guys a little younger, so that it made sense that she could kind of intimidate them, boss them around. But to make that work, we had to make them so young, Sam said we might as well put fucking school uniforms on them. And he was joking, but the executives said, well you know, that's a pretty good idea, some kind of uniform, because then you can tell at a glance that they're a gang, and not just a bunch of hobos, because they didn't like the way Sam dressed his characters, they weren't what you might call photogenic. I mean, posters for his films looked like Wanted For Vagrancy posters.

So now we had a movie about a nun looking after a bunch of kids and I said, Sam, I think this is getting away from us a little here. But Sam, he said, look, we can turn it around on the set. We'll head out to Mexico, get away from the suits, and shoot this right. But the producers get wind of this, and they say we can't shoot in Mexico. And he says, there's no suitable locations in the US. Which is bullshit, but they call his bluff and say OK then, we'll shoot it overseas in the cheapest location we can find, what do you need? He says, sunshine, hills. They go looking and it turns out that the Austrian government is trying to build up a film industry in what they call its 'disadvantaged regions', so we can get major, major tax breaks if we shoot about a mile up in the Alps. Sam goes through the fucking ceiling, but the producers say, look, you asked for hills and sunshine, what's the problem? Yeah, Sam says, OK, there's sunshine because we're above the fucking clouds. I can't shoot this script in the fucking Alps. But by this time they're getting pissed off with Sam, and the Austrian government has sweetened the deal even more, they're desperate for a big Hollywood production, so the producers dig in and say, then change the fucking script. So we change the fucking script and set it in Austria, with a bunch of European deadbeats hiding out in the mountains. And Sam thinks, well, fuck it, let's make the best of this, and he says, seeing as we're setting it in Austria, we can make the guys hunting the gang Nazis. The producers say fine, although the Austrian government isn't crazy about this.

Now around this time this woman, calls herself the Singing Nun, has a huge hit with this terrible song, 'Dominique'. And the marketing department say, look, singing nuns are huge right now – I mean, this is the way these idiots think – can we have our nun sing a song maybe and they can release it as a single a couple of months before the movie opens, build up some word of mouth. Typical marketing bullshit. And we're, come on, you think a singing nun is going to bring in kids to a Western like *The Wild Bunch*? And they say, hey, Clint Eastwood is singing in *Paint Your Wagon*, and Lee Marvin too, if you can call it singing, don't get pissy here, there ain't nothing wrong with singing cowboys. So we let them have the song.

I think it was at this point Sam really started to worry. I mean, Sam was good with the suits, and he was good with bullshit, but this was too much bullshit even for him to deal with, so he starts talking to another studio on the side, about switching the project over to them. But they'd just got in some ex-Disney exec as head of production – some coke-sniffing wife-beater who liked whores to shit on his chest – anyway, full of family values, and he's all, the Nazis will scare the kids, what if they were, say, foxes? And what if the nun was a rabbit? And, you know, we could animate it. And Sam says no fucking way, so the new head of production tries another angle and now he's all, we like the Wild Bunch, we really like these guys, but sometimes it can be hard to tell them apart. Maybe give each of them a characteristic, you know, some little thing that they do in every scene. This one is a little stupid, this one has hayfever, this one falls asleep real easy, you know. So that's how you got that version of the script with Dopey and Sneezy and so on . . . But Sam nixed that side deal after the guy wanted us to end the film with a miracle, to bring the Catholics and the National Legion of Decency onside. So we went back to Warner Brothers. Better the devil you know. And casting, casting was a nightmare, because the English actress they'd signed up to play the tough nun, when she turned up she looked even younger than her age, so we kept casting the Wild Bunch younger and younger. Sam tried to get all his old gang on board, but there was just no way. I remember Warren Oates with his busted nose and one ear shot away, literally dropping to his knees in front of Sam and saying 'I can play sixteen, going on seventeen!' And because we were fighting with the casting director every day, we took our eye off the Wardrobe Department, which was a mistake. So, by the end of the casting process, the Wild Bunch were a gang of little kids in fucking sailor suits, and a sexy nun. Now Sam's pretty far gone at this stage, so he just groans and says yeah, sure, whatever, and he goes home and he shoots tin cans off his fence till it gets dark.

So we get out to Austria, and the first day goes fine, Sam's knocking it out of the park, gets through twenty-three camera setups, the hills are alive with the sound of gunfire. But, second day, the Austrians come out to the set and say, hey, we have very strict laws in Austria about replica firearms and explosives, and the fuckers took all our guns and pyrotechnics. So we had to rewrite on the set. No gun battles, no robberies, so we gave more songs to the kids to give them something to do. Sam was so heartbroken by the last day, he just handed all the footage over to the editor, told the studio do what they liked with it.

When it was all over I tried to console Sam. I said look, you've made a great film, at least it's still about the Nazis chasing a gang over the mountains. But just before release, the studio changed the title, and that was the last straw. Sam took his name off the film. He was sure it was going to be a disaster. Well, you know, it made Julie Andrews a star, it made over a billion dollars in today's money, won five Oscars, won Best Picture. He never even went to see it. I still think it's Sam's best film. But that's show business.

Those Who Remember

NIGHT HAD FALLEN when I reached Oldbury. The best time for coming home: when the new developments fade into the background and the past becomes real again. Over the years I'd seen expressways carve up the landscape and titanic, jerry-built tower blocks loom above the familiar terraces. The town was boxed in by industrial estates built on the sites of old factories. Instead of real things like steel and brick, the new businesses manufactured 'office space' and 'electronics'. Only the night could make me feel at home. The night and seeing Dean again.

He took some finding this time. The windows of his old house were boarded up, and two short planks had been nailed across the front door: one at the top, one at the bottom. If they'd been nailed together, I could believe it was still his home. It was hard to imagine him leaving the area, but maybe he was dead or in prison.

I walked around the streets for hours. Everything had changed except the people. The teenagers had designer tops and mobile phones now, but they fought in car parks and fucked in alleys just as they had when I was a teenager. Local industry was dying then; it was dead now. Opposite a new multi-storey car park, I saw the old cinema where

Dean and I had gone to see *Butch Cassidy and the Sundance Kid* when we were twelve. The doorway and windows were bricked up.

The next morning, I checked the phone book. Dean was living in one of the tower blocks north of the town centre. Where the council stuck people who had, or were, problems. It saved the social services a lot of petrol. I could see the towers from my hostel room: three grey rectangles cut out of the white sky. Gulls flying around them like flakes of ash, probably drawn by the heaps of rubbish on the slope.

I walked through the town, past the drive-in McDonald's that was now its chief landmark. A narrow estate, with tiny cube-shaped flats in rows three or four deep, seemed to be in process of demolition: half of the cubes were broken up, their blank interiors exposed to the weak morning light. It had been much the same three years earlier. I try to come back every now and then, without letting Dean know my plans. I prefer to surprise him. At least the wasteground with the remains of a derelict house, where he and his mates Wayne and Richard had beaten me senseless in 1979, was still here. I walked through it, glancing around for the teeth I'd lost. One day they'd turn up.

Climbing the bare hill to the three towers, I passed a few children who were stoning an old van. They'd taken out most of the windscreen. I waited at the entrance to the second tower until a young woman dressed in black came out; I slipped in past her. It seemed colder inside the building than outside; the stone steps reeked of piss and cleaning fluids. Dean's flat was on the ninth floor. While climbing, I rehearsed what I was going to make him do.

After ten minutes of ringing, the door finally opened. He was looking rough, less than half awake. The kind of piecemeal shave that's worse than none at all. Shadows like old bruises round his eyes, which were flecked with blood. 'What are you after?' he said. 'I don't feel too good. Come back later.'

'Not a chance.' I took his shaky hand off the door and pushed it further open, then walked in. The smell of despair washed over me: three parts sweat, two parts stale food and booze, one part something like burnt plastic. The curtains were shut. I raised a hand. 'Miss Havisham, I have returned – to let in the light!'

Dean laughed. 'Gary, have you seen the view?' He probably had a point. I shifted a few dusty magazines to make space on the couch, then sat down. 'It's been a long time,' he said. 'Why have you come back? I don't need you.'

'Yeah, you're doing just fine on your own.' I looked around his living-room. Boxes and suitcases were stacked against the far wall, under a stain like a deformed spider. 'Have you just moved in, or are you leaving?'

It took him a while to get the point. 'Been here a couple of years,' he said. 'Lost my job, tried to sell the house but it needed too much work. Council found me this flat. It'll do while I get myself sorted out.'

'Sure.' The burnt plastic smell was troubling me. 'Have you had a short circuit or something? Cable burning out?'

Again, he had to think for a bit. 'I was cooking up some breakfast.'

'Excellent. Haven't had a bacon butty in ages.'

'Oh, I've put it all away now. In case . . .' His eyes closed.

I stood up wearily and walked over to him, looked closely at his face. His eyes opened again; he looked away. 'Dean, there were three things you could never keep. A promise, a bank account and a secret. What is it this time?'

'Nothing.' He put a hand to his mouth, then staggered. 'Fuck.'

'I'd rather have a coffee to start with.'

Dean gave me a look of utter contempt, then staggered through a side door. I could hear him throwing up in the toilet. The magazines on the couch were his usual blend of soft porn, war and the paranormal. He came back after a minute, looking sweaty. 'Need to go out for a while,' he said.

'Sit down first. I want to talk to you.' He shrugged and balanced his lean arse on a plastic chair. 'Have you done any work since you moved here?'

'Building . . . sometimes. More demo than building. It's all casual now, you take what you can get.' I remembered he'd started a one-man repair firm in his twenties. Hadn't lasted long. He'd kept a horse tethered to his gate.

'What about Richard and Wayne? Do you still work for them?'

I saw a flicker of recognition in his eyes. Maybe he was starting to remember. 'I never worked for them,' he said. 'Just the odd bit of business. You know?' I nodded. 'Look, I need to go out now. Got a job interview.'

He was wearing a torn grey fabric top, stained jeans and trainers without laces. They might have had a certain urchin appeal if he'd been sixteen instead of forty-one. But he'd always been sixteen to me, so it didn't matter. An employer might feel differently.

I reached out, gripped his hand. It felt cold and thin. I pulled his sleeve back to the elbow and saw the tracks. He didn't try to stop me. He was drifting off again. 'Dean, I'm going to help you,' I said. 'And that means you're not going anywhere for a while. Tough love. We'll get through this together. And afterwards, I need you to help me.'

Dean leaned forward and held onto the wall. A thin stream of drool ran from the corner of his mouth. Then, suddenly, he ran for the door. I stopped him. 'Fuck off, fuck off, fuck off,' he kept repeating. I held him until he curled up on the floor, his hands over his head, and went to sleep.

The next three days were hard work. I took Dean's keys and kept the flat locked. He wasn't that likely to jump out the window from the ninth floor. A search of his bedroom revealed a battered set of works, a couple of syringes and a plastic bag with few meagre traces of powder. I destroyed all of it. While he was asleep I slipped out to buy bread, milk and bleach, then cleaned the flat as best I could. While he was awake I listened to his rantings, his promises and threats, his explanations and frantic pleas. I cleaned him when he shat and threw up over himself. I wiped the sickly, malodorous sweat from his face and body. And yes, I gave him a couple of handjobs when he became aroused. I have to take some gratification where I can find it. Though I got rather more pleasure from throwing his mobile phone out the window, not even hearing it strike the gravel far below.

After three days, I decided he'd got through the 'cold turkey' and was ready for the next stage. Of course, he'd only keep off the smack with ongoing support to help him fight the craving. But to be honest, that wasn't my concern. He was always in trouble: the last time it had been diazepam, and a couple of times before that he'd been drinking himself blind. I always did what I could to clean him up, put him back on the path. But he'd never had much sense. Like some historian said, those who forget the past are condemned to repeat it.

And those who remember do it anyway.

When I gave Dean back his keys, he was a different man. His clothes were washed and he'd had a healthy breakfast. His flat was still a dump, but it was a cleaner dump that smelt only of pine-scented bleach. He smiled at me, and I could almost have kissed him. 'Now I need you to do something for me,' I said. He waited. 'First we're going out for a decent coffee. Then I want you to find Wayne and Richard. And help me kill them.'

Dean made the call from an infected phone box on the estate of broken cubes. Said he was clean but had debts to pay. He wasn't kidding. Richard said Wayne was away cutting some overgrown grass. He'd be back tomorrow. They could meet in the usual place. That was the derelict house, Dean explained to me; or rather what was left of it. I was touched to realise I wasn't the only person trapped in the past. The death of religion has left us all to create our own rituals.

We walked out past the Homebase to the new junction, a twisted structure gleaming with light. The gateway to the future. Cars streamed above us as I explained to Dean what he was going to do. 'It's not just what they did to me,' I said. 'You'll never have a decent life while they're around. They know far too much about you. That's why you can't leave this shithole. It has to end. Ten seconds and we'll both be free. Then I'll leave you alone.'

He stared at me in a confused way. The years of alcohol and drugs had taken their toll. And he'd hardly been the brightest light on the tree to begin with. 'There's no other way,' I said, and handed him the knife. He touched his finger to the blade, licked the blood off his fingertip. Then he turned the knife over and over in his hands, gazing at it. I think he knew where it had come from, but I moved us on before he could think too much.

'I need money for a new mobile,' he said as we walked back through the town. I had no idea what they cost, but took fifty quid from my old wallet and handed it to him. We passed a branch of Dixon's, but he didn't stop. He was trembling. For a moment I could see him as a teenager, walking up that mountainside in North Wales.

As we neared the estate, I asked him: 'What about that mobile?'

'I need a date first,' he said without looking at me. 'Now I'm off drugs, I've got the urge back. There's a girl on the fourteenth floor of my block. She'll do everything for fifty. Tomorrow could go wrong, Gary. I deserve it.'

'You always were the romantic type.' I briefly considered just pushing his face through a window. But that wouldn't be enough. 'I'll leave you to it, Romeo. Be outside your block tomorrow morning at twelve. Or fucking else.'

The town streets were jammed with traffic, workers on their lunch break, pensioners hunting for cheap food. The air was getting warmer, but I was too cold inside to derive much comfort from that. I bought a four-pack of Diamond White, took it back to my hostel room and drank off all the bottles without a break. Thinking about the derelict house: four shattered walls, a few heaps of timber, flakes of plaster, exposed wires. Then I thought of some tents on a hillside in Wales, stars glittering in the open sky like flaws in ice. Finally I drew the curtains, lay down and pretended to sleep. That was the only way I could make myself think of nothing.

'I'm not doing it.' He was wearing a battered leather jacket, but still shivering. The sky behind the three tower blocks was the grey of dead skin. He cupped his thin hands and blew into them, shaking his head.

'Are you back on the fucking horse?'

'No, I told you, a date. She fucking loved it.'

'Spare me,' I said. 'The most romantic thing a girl's ever said to you is *Is it in yet?*'

Dean gazed down the hill at the shattered boxes where people had lived. Where they maybe still did. 'They're my mates,' he said. 'What do you know about friendship?'

'I know a gayboy when I see one.'

'Why, you look in the mirror? I like women.'

'Gail didn't love it, did she?'

He looked at me then, confusion and panic in his face. 'What are you talking about?'

'I'm talking about the one chance you've got to show you're a man. A human being of any kind. Those two don't deserve to walk the streets, and you know it. Or are you just going to spend the rest of your useless life in that derelict house, the two of them taking turns to come in your mouth?'

He started walking down the hill towards the estate. 'Don't need a fucking syringe, do I? You never give up jabbing the needle in.'

At the edge of the wasteground, he stopped again. 'Can't see them. They're going to jump on us.'

'You wish.' I was losing patience. 'I'm with you, remember. It's two against two. I know you prefer three against one. But we've got the advantage. Let's get this over with, for fuck's sake.' I shoved him forward. 'Loser. Coward. Fairy. Don't you know what the knife is for? You used to.'

He walked on fast over the wet, uneven ground. The remains of the derelict house were on the far side: a black-ened structure only four or five feet high, with part of an empty window-frame in one broken wall. The doorway had long since collapsed, and you had to climb over the crumbling bricks to get through. There was no longer any roof. Two figures were waiting on either side of the few mouldering stairs. They'd put on some weight.

'Who's this fucker?' I wasn't sure if it was Wayne or Richard speaking.

'I think you know,' Dean said quietly. 'He's been here before.'

'You're fucking kidding,' the other one said. Dean whipped the knife out of his coat pocket, gave a wordless cry, and charged at him.

Richard, I think it was, kicked him hard in the stomach. Wayne grabbed his right arm and snapped the wrist with a single carefully aimed karate chop. The knife dropped soundlessly onto the rotting stairs. Dean fell to his knees and vomited. I stood outside the ruin, watching through the empty window-frame.

The two men worked him over for a couple of minutes, doing no serious damage, but inflicting as much pain as they could. They left him lying on his back, twitching and drooling blood. As an afterthought, Wayne pissed over him. Then they walked out without glancing in my direction. They walked away fast, as if they had other business to attend to.

It took Dean an hour to regain consciousness. Bruising had closed his left eye, and blood had crusted over his mouth. He looked like a poorly made-up circus clown. He lifted his right arm and moaned with pain. Then he saw me standing inside the half-wall, watching him. All his memories were coming back. 'What's wrong?' I asked. 'Don't you like it that way?'

His damaged mouth tried to say something, but I couldn't tell what. 'Why don't you finish it?' I said. 'I'll let you off the fuck this time. They beat you up too much. Just use the knife.' I picked it up and wiped the flecks of plaster from the handle, then put it in his left hand. Dean struggled to his knees. I slipped off my jacket, turned my back to him and put my hands on the window-frame.

The knife went in between my ribs, just to the right of the spine. It was more a carving than a stabbing action. My back arched in the ecstasy of release. I saw my last breath like a scar on the petrol-tinged air. The knife struck me again, but the tissues of my body were already corroding and flaking apart, the bones melting like ice in spring. By the time he let go of the knife and began his long, painful walk to the town, there was nothing left of me.

Dean was the only one of the three who went on the camping trip to Wales where we climbed a mountain and put up cheap tents in a sloping field. I shared a tent with a boy called Alan. In the night some of the boys visited the girls' tents. I just lay there, pretending to sleep.

Long after midnight, someone crept in through the tent-flap. It wasn't Alan, who'd gone out an hour before: it was Dean. He told me Gail, the red-haired girl, had refused him. 'I'm not good enough for her. So I thought, I know who I'm good enough for.'

He fucked me slowly, without spit or tenderness. Afterwards he lay there as if stunned. I asked: 'Aren't you going to finish me off?'

He laughed as if I'd made a joke, then grabbed my arm. 'Come with me.' We got dressed and left the tent. I'd never seen night outside the city before, couldn't believe how bright the stars were. Dean led me to a footpath that curved away from the field into a wooded area that reached up the mountainside. It was midsummer, but I felt cold. His sperm was trickling into my underpants. I no longer wanted any reciprocal contact. But I kept walking until the footpath led us out of the trees to a ridge overlooking a steep rock face and a tree-lined valley. 'Stop here,' he said.

I turned to face him. He was breathing heavily, and wouldn't meet my eyes. 'You want me to finish you off?' I didn't answer. 'Turn round.'

A terrible chill spread from between my shoulder-blades through my whole body. The knife stayed in my back as I fell towards the dark trees. I was still alive when I hit the ground, and for hours afterwards. But nobody found me. Nobody ever found me, or the knife.

That's another reunion done with. I'll be back next year, or the year after, or a couple of years after that. I like to surprise him. But the scene is decaying. Maybe next time they'll kill him. Or else he'll kill himself, with drugs or booze if not with violence. Nothing lasts for ever, and there's no eternal. Everything falls apart in the end.

STELLA DUFFY

To Brixton Beach

T HERE ARE IMAGES in the water. The pool holds them, has held them, since it was built in the thirties and before. And before that too, when there were ponds here, in the park, ponds the locals used to bathe in. Men at first, then men and women, separate bathing times, of course. A pond before the pool, a house with gardens before the park, perhaps a common before that, a field, a forest. We can go back for ever. And on, and on.

6 a.m. The first swimmers arrive, absurd to the gym-goers, the yoga-bunnies, those impatient, imperfect bodies readying for the cold, clear, cool.

When Charlie was a boy he and his brother Sid used to run all the way up from Kennington to swim, skipping out in the middle of the night, long hot summer nights, too sweaty in their little room, no mother there to watch over them anyway, sneaking off on their mate Bill's bike, to where the air was fresher, the trees greener, the sky and stars deeper, wider. And the pond so clean, green. Charlie hadn't been to the sea or to the mountains then, but the air in Brockwell Park felt cool enough.

8 a.m., the pre-office rush, pushing at the entrance desk, swimmers to the right, gym-ers to the left, one half

to fast breath, hot body, pumping music, the other to cold, cool, clear.

Mid-morning and the local kids begin to arrive. Jayneen lives in the Barrier Block, in summer she and her friend Elise and Elise's cousin Monique go to the lido every day. They walk along streets named for poets, poets Monique has read too, poets she knows, smart girl, smart mouth an all, they walk in tiny shorts and tinier tops and they know what they do, and they laugh as they do it, as those boys slow down on the foolish too-small bikes they ride, slow down and look them up, look them lower, look them over. They three are all young woman skin and flesh showing and body ripe. And they know it, love it. The girls walk along and make their way to the lido that is Brixton Beach and they don't bother getting changed, they are not here to swim, Elise spent five hours last weekend getting her hair made fine in rows, tight and fine, she doesn't want to risk chlorine on that, they come to the lido to sit and soak up the sun and the admiring glances. Jayneen looks around, smoothing soft cocoa butter on her skin, as she does twice a day, every day, as she knows to do, and sucks her teeth at the skinny white girl over there by the café, all freckles and burned red, burned dry, silly sitting in the sun. Jayneen's skin is smooth and soft, she's taught Monique too, white girls need to oil their skin too. Maybe white girls need black mothers to teach them how to take care of themselves.

Charlie is in the water. He is already always in the water. Strong powerful strokes pulling him through. He slips past the young men who are running and cartwheeling into the pool, trying to get the girls' attention, trying not to get the life guard's attention, paying no attention to the long low deco lines. The young men look only at the curving lines on young women's bodies. Charlie finds himself thinking of young women and turns his attention back to water, to swimming hard and remembering how to breathe in water. He swims fast and strong up to the shallow end, avoids the squealing, screeching little ones, babes in arms, and turns back, to power on down, alone.

Lunchtime, the place is full. Midday office escapees, retired schoolteachers and half of Brixton market, rolled up Railton Road to get to the green, the water, the blue. One end of the café's outdoor tables over-taken with towels and baby bottles and children's soft toys, floating girls and boys in the water with the yummy mummies, wet mummies, hold me mummy, hold me.

Two babies hanging on to each arm. Helen can't believe it. This is not what she'd planned when she booked that first maternity leave, four years ago. Can it really be so long? She looks at her left hand where Sophia and her play-date Cassandra jump up and down, pumping her arm for dear life (dear god, who calls their daughter Cassandra? Foretelling the doom of the south London middle classes), while in her right arm she rocks the little rubber ring that Gideon and Katsuki hang on to. Helen shakes her head. Back in the day. Back in the office, loving those days in the office, she wondered what it would feel like, to be one of them, the East Dulwich mummies clogging cafés and footpaths with their designer buggies. She looks up as a shadow crosses her, it is Imogen, Cassandra's mother. Imogen is pointing to the table, surrounded by buggies. Their friends wave, lunch has arrived, Helen passes the children out one by one and immediately they start whining, wanting this, wanting that, she can feel the looks, the disapproval from the swimmers who have come here for quiet and peace. Helen has become that mother. The one with the designer buggy. And she hates the lookers for making her feel it, and hates that she feels it. And she wouldn't give her up babies for anything. And they do need a buggy, and a big one at that, they're twins. (At least she didn't call them Castor and Pollux.) Helen can't win and she knows it. Sits down to her veggie burger. Orders a glass of wine anyway. After all.

Charlie swims, back and forth, back and forth. He lurches into the next lane to avoid the young men dive-bombing to impress the girls and irritate the life guards, makes his perfect turns between two young women squealing at the cold water. He swerves around slower swimmers, through groups of chattering children, he does not stop. Charlie is held in the water, only in the water.

3 p.m., a mid-afternoon lull. Margaret and Esther sit against the far wall, in direct sunlight, they have been here for five hours, moving to follow the sun. From inside the yoga studio they can hear the slow in and out breaths, the sounds of bodies pulled and pushed into perfection. At seventy-six and eighty-one Margaret and Esther do not worry about perfection, though Margaret still has good legs and Esther is proud of her full head of per-fectly white hair. Margaret looks down at her body, the sagging and whole right breast, the missing left. She had the mastectomy fifteen years ago, they spoke to her about reconstruction, but she wasn't much interested, nor in the prosthesis. Margaret likes her body as it is, scars, white hair, wrinkles, lived. She and Esther have been coming to the pool every summer, three times a week for fifty years, bar that bad patch when the council closed it in the 80s. They swim twenty lengths together, heads above the water, a slow breaststroke side by side because Esther likes to chat and keep her lovely hair dry. Then Esther gets out and Margaret swims another twenty herself, head down this time, breathing out in the water, screaming out in the water sometimes, back then, when it was harder,

screaming in the water because it was the only time Esther couldn't hear her cry. It's better now, she is alive and delighted to be here, glad to be sharing another summer with the love of her life. Esther passes her a slice of ginger cake, buttered, and they sit back to watch the water. Two old ladies, holding age-spotted hands.

Charlie swims on.

5.30 p.m., just before the after-office rush. In the changing rooms, Ameena takes a deep breath as she unwraps her swimming costume from her towel. She sent away for it a week ago, when she knew she could no longer deny herself the water. It arrived yesterday. It is a beautiful, deep blue. It makes her think of water even to touch it, the texture is soft, silky. She has been hot for days, wants to give herself over to the water, to the pool. She slowly takes off her own clothes and replaces them as she does with the deep blue costume. When she has dressed in the two main pieces – swim pants and tunic – she goes to the mirror to pull on the hood, fully covering her hair. Three little girls stand and stare unashamedly. She smiles at them and takes the bravery of their stare for herself, holds her covered head high, walks through the now-quiet changing room, eyes glancing her way, conversations lowered, walks out to the pool in her deep blue burkini. Ameena loved swimming at school, has been denying herself the water since she decided to dress in full hijab. She does not want to deny herself any more. The burkini is her choice, the water her desire. She can have both, and will brave the stares to do so. In the water, Ameena looks like any other woman in a wetsuit, swims better than most, and gives herself over to the repetitive mantra that are her arms and legs, heart and lungs, working in unison. It is almost prayer and she is grateful.

Charlie swims two, three, four lengths in time with

Ameena, and then their rhythm changes, one is out of sync with the other, they are separate again.

8 p.m., the café is almost full, the pool almost empty, a last few swimmers, defying the imploring calls of the lifeguards. Time to close up, time to get out. Diners clink wine glasses and look through fairy lights past the lightly stirring water to the gym, people on treadmills, on step machines, in ballet and spinning classes. Martin and Ayo order another beer each and shake their heads. They chose food and beer tonight. And will probably do so again tomorrow evening, they are well matched, well met.

It is quiet and dark night. Charlie swims on, unnoticed. Eventually the café is closed, the gym lights turned off, the cleaners have been and gone, the pool and the park are silent but for the foxes telling the night, tolling the hours with their screams. And a cat, watching.

Charlie climbs from the water now, his body his own again, reassembled from the wishing and the tears and the could be, might be, would be, from hope breathed out into water, from the grins of young men and the laughter of old women and the helpless, rolling giggles of toddlers on soft towels. Remade through summer laughter spilling over the poolside. He dresses. White shirt, long pants, baggy trousers falling over his toes, a waistcoat, tie just-spotted, just-knotted below the turned-up collar, then the too-tight jacket, his big shoes. Without the cane and the moustache and the bowler hat he was just another man, moving at his own pace, quietly through the water. With them, he is himself again. The Little Tramp walking away, back to Kennington, retracing the path he and Sid ran through summer nights to the welcome ponds of Brockwell Park.

Behind him the water holds the memory of a man

moving through it in cool midnight, a celluloid pool in which he flickers to life, and is gone.

SOCRATES ADAMS

Wide and Deep

I AM FIVE and a half years old. I am holding my wife's hand as she gives birth to our son. My wife is six years old. I am her toy boy. The nurse, who is eight years old, is saying things to my wife like, 'Keep pushing. You are nearly there.' I keep hold of my wife's hand even though she is gripping me as hard as she can. My fingers are white as my son is born. The nurse places the tiny boy into my wife's arms and she starts to breastfeed him, automatically. I am swelling with pride.

I feel a triangle of love. The triangle is connecting my wife, the baby, me. The triangle seems like a beam of green light, made of love.

My wife is crying as she breastfeeds the baby. The family I have is the greatest family in the history of families. I imagine my son's life, stretching out in front of me, and I am immeasurably happy.

My son is two weeks old and it is time for him to go to school. My son's first words were 'Feed me'. He said the words and then my wife/his mother started to immediately feed him. Whenever she feeds him she is so overcome with emotion that she cries. She doesn't stop crying maybe for one or two hours after she feeds him. Then she feeds him again.

I drive to the school and I talk to my son as we drive along. I tell him about school being an important place. My son quietly sits and thinks about the big issues of life. When we get to the school the headteacher is waiting for my son and she takes him and moves him into the school. I worry about my son suffering from separation anxiety.

When I get home my wife is standing in the corner of the kitchen. She is facing the corner and crying. I go upstairs and work because I have taken my work home with me.

My wife and I are at my son's first birthday party. His friends are here. He is about to cut his cake and pop open the champagne and drink it with them and then go out on the town. I look at my wife who is looking at the cake. We are both proud of my son and each other. I think about the way I have changed since he was born. I think about the way my wife has changed. My wife is a tiny and thin creature.

My wife collapses onto the floor, silently. My son and his friends have a great time drinking the champagne and cutting the cake. I lie down on the floor next to my wife and whisper to her quietly as the boys trample on top of us. I look at her face and it is drawn and pale. I touch her face with my hand and keep whispering to her.

It is three months since the party. We are at the graveyard and we are burying my wife. I have found it difficult since she died. I rely on my son now. When I look at him I can often imagine her older face. I am six and three-quarters years old. My son is one and one-quarter years old. My wife would be seven and one-quarter years old. My son's

93

girlfriend comes up to me after the funeral and says to me that my wife had a good innings. My son's girlfriend is one and two-thirds years old.

I can rely on my son. He and his girlfriend leave me at the church. I sit on the bench in the graveyard and I squeeze my hand and make it white and remember about my wife giving birth to my son.

I live in an old people's home. I am totally mad because of my dementia. I don't understand human emotions/responsibilities/family structures any more. I sit in a rocking chair on the lawn. I watch a ten-year-old shuffle along the lawn and fall down dead. I start singing the song that I sing every day:

dig me my grave both wide and deep
put marble slabs at my head and feet
upon my breast put a turtle white dove
to show the whole world that I died of love

JO LLOYD

Tarnished Sorry Open

THE BIG ROOM is not made for sleep. There are no curtains on the windows and the blinds are never drawn. It is lit at night by the overspill of light intended for other purposes. The white beams trained on the fire station yard three floors below, the steady orange glow of streetlamps along the narrow residential roads, the fleeting, inward gleams of houses and flats, blinking on and off as children wake, old men stumble to the bathroom, lone revellers unlock their doors to the cold company of late night TV. And from above, the dim haze of stars and planets, satellites, and sometimes, brighter than everything else, the slow turning mirror of the moon. In this muddled carnival dusk the machines wait all night, not sleeping, and hum, as if the fortuitous light has provoked their chorus. The heat rises off them and hangs in a thick tide, swirling over the desks and rolling up against the ceiling tiles. Only the server room is cool. The machines sequestered in there will work until they fail and then they will be patched up with spare bits of RAM, a new hard drive, to work some more. When they are beyond economic repair they will be dismantled, any viable parts removed, the rest wiped and tossed. They will live out their short lives of unceasing work without ever seeing the moon or the stars or the firefighters running across the yard pulling on their uniforms.

Patrick is the first to arrive. The doors admit him with a sigh and the strip lights, as he walks down the corridor, bang into life, flicker, then settle to a high-pitched whine that eight or ten years before he might have been able to hear. Not looking left or right or out of the window, he heads straight to his desk on the far side of the big room, turns on the screen, and starts going through the team jobs. Accumulated errors scroll rapidly in front of him, filling the screen, running off the top.

They are stupid mistakes for the most part. Every day Patrick is surprised again, as if for the first time, by his colleagues' carelessness. Bad joins. Sloppy casting. Their minds somewhere else, committing their half-done work with a shrug, as if the system will accommodate their mis-constructions. He will return these tasks as if they are part of a long-running joke, pointing out a ridiculous infer-ence, a blunder a child of ten would have spotted. He will laugh about it. Sometimes the culprit, even, will allow a grudging smile.

Then there are the deep, intractable errors, subtle and randomly manifesting, that must be traced carefully backwards through the code. Errors that, when Patrick manages finally to track them to their source, will be greeted by the developers with awe, as if they prove the operation of some whimsical force stronger than logic.

Patrick himself hardly ever commits an error.

As he works, people start to arrive, singly at first, cross-ing the hushed room in silence, heads bowed, then in twos and threes and fours, yawning and sighing. Patrick glances up as colleagues settle at neighbouring stations. They have been up late again, drinking. They are pale.

There are creases under their eyes where they have slept heavily, their faces crushed against the mattress. They will do their work badly. They will make more silly mistakes.

Often they go out drinking together, after work, after he has left. To mark birthdays, engagements, new jobs, new contracts, the end of a week, the end of a day. They have shorthand for the pubs, an email will go around. 5.30 – *you know where,* it will say. Or *Usual time, Tuesday place. Everyone welcome.*

Patrick sees Antony, almost last to arrive, picking his way to his desk cautiously, as if the floor is uneven. He has had to reopen one of Antony's tasks. Not for anything critical, but something that could have been done more elegantly. It did not occur to Patrick that it might be to his advantage to let it pass, just this once, just for today.

The office falls quiet. Eyes patrol their square foot of screen, fingers hurrying in the shadows below. All over the big room, code is being stripped down, patched up, decisions preordained, judgements rendered implacable.

By the time Patrick goes to the kitchen for his mid-morning coffee, people are properly awake. They have deleted, responded, prevaricated, fixed some errors, made a few more. They shrug, unpenitent. They can feel the weekend coming, a shift in the weight of the air. Today is just a corridor to be passed through.

In the kitchen, Antony and Doug are standing near the coffee maker. Patrick sees his chance. They have their coffee, but seem in no hurry to leave. Antony is telling a funny story. And not even fifth gear, he says, and Doug laughs. Not even fourth! They are both laughing.

Patrick, approaching, stopping, laughs too. He stands with his hands in his pockets, looking from one to the other, and laughs. They look at him, move aside.

Morning Patrick. Sorry, are we in your way?

No, no, it's alright, he says, staying where he is, rocking on his heels.

But they wait and he has to move.

He pours a coffee. He will say something now, he thinks. But their talk has closed around them. When Doug is talking Antony is saying Mmm mmm, and nodding. When Antony is talking Doug is laughing, saying Yes, that's right. There is no way in. He has to pick up his coffee, walk past them. There is no reason to stop, halfway down the kitchen, mug in hand. No reason he can come up with. He has to leave, go back to his desk.

His screen has turned its gaze, in his absence, onto the expanding universe, stars hurrying towards their extinction. Later, he thinks. There will be another chance. He must watch out for Antony. He touches the mouse and the galaxies dissolve into rows of badly done code.

When he has finished with the testing jobs, he turns to his own tasks. He will finish them in half the time estimated. As each task is completed he will pick up the next. He never looks beyond that.

Every year, in his review, Patrick's managers tell him how much they depend on him. His speed, his accuracy, his productivity. Every year the same thing, only the words varying as one manager is replaced by the next, even younger. These new managers have degrees in business or economics, they could not write a single line of code. They talk about team skills, client interfacing, adding value. They look down at their sheets of paper. Look up again. These are difficult times, they say. Patrick smiles politely. They frown at him. Anyway, they say, keep doing what you're doing. We depend on you.

His colleagues cannot come close. They trudge through their work, sighing, they get things wrong, get them wrong again, miss deadlines, their tasks have to be reassigned. They are distracted by dates and dinner parties, by the girlfriends with blouses and lipstick that save their screens.

This will not happen to Patrick. His approach is too orderly to be undermined by the changes that are about to take place, the more comfortable home life that will soon, finally, be his.

At twelve o'clock he eats at his desk. The tupperware box signals to anyone who might think of approaching that he is on his lunch. He unpeels the foil around the sandwich he made that morning. Cheese and tomato. He reads while he eats, technical sites, industry news. There is nothing, today, of particular interest or surprise. Afterwards he eats a Kit Kat.

He remembers Antony. But when he goes to the kitchen to make a cup of tea there is only Milly from admin there. She is leaning against the wall, texting. She raises her eyelashes momentarily and he nods at her. She will know, he realises, he can ask her.

He puts the kettle on, trying to piece together an opening line. He does not find Milly easy to talk to. She giggles. She makes extravagant gestures. She shakes out her hair, raising her arms above her head so that her breasts rise towards him like waves breaking over a jetty.

But she is in his debt. More than once, he has helped her cover up stupid things she has done. There was that time she messed up her files and lost the budgets. And the time she put a virus on the server, doing something she shouldn't have been doing at work. He could bring that up. Although it is only what anyone would expect from admin, nothing to do all day but play solitaire and Twitter. Perhaps that is not the place to start. He will say something about the weekend. About how soon it will be here.

When he turns around to speak to her, Milly has left the room.

He lingers over making his tea, thinking she might come back, someone is sure to come in, but when someone does it is one of the new people, someone with a haircut and shoes, he can't even remember the name. He goes back to his desk.

His calendar surfaces, beeps discreetly. He has clients in that afternoon. More time wasted. He will have to stop in the middle of this task to try and explain table constraints to people who've never heard of third normal.

When Patrick goes to the meeting room, Rav has already set the demo up, is flicking through the headlines while he waits.

We should run through the new section, says Patrick.

It's cool, says Rav. I tried it earlier.

Patrick has never been able to see why his managers have to put some fool like Rav in with him. He can handle these things perfectly well on his own. But this afternoon, Rav will, for once, be useful. Time is running out.

It was Rav who started this, at the last meeting. They had been left waiting again. Rav was fidgeting as usual, tilting his chair back, yawning, probably hung over.

You going to Antony's party? Rav had said.

I'm busy, Patrick had said. It was his standard response, although at that point he had not known when the party was.

I've been to a couple now, said Rav. No, three. They're wild. I've never seen so many girls in one place. I swear. So many girls. How does he know them even?

Patrick looked at him.

He's a dark one, said Rav. Pretty girls too. Not dogs. I don't know where he finds them. You can't go?

Afraid not.

I think he pays for them. That's what I think. He buys them in for the evening. From Poland or somewhere. A lorry load of girls.

This was a joke. Patrick laughed.

You should see it, Rav said. In the house, in the garden, lying around on the lawn. They're everywhere, under your feet, like, I don't know, kittens.

Patrick's thoughts flitted for a moment to the frosty women on dating sites, with their bad spelling and unreasonable expectations.

It's just wild, Rav went on. Draped all over the place. Just everywhere. I mean you'll be walking around and you'll trip over some girl asleep under a table.

The conversation has stayed in Patrick's mind, has grown and filled, coming into focus, first pixels here and there, then tessellated shapes, an eye, a hand, recognisable figures. The picture is sharp now, detailed, almost as if he knows Antony's house, has been to his parties. He can see Antony and Rav, Doug and Milly. He can see the rooms, the tables, the girls under them. He can almost, now, see himself there, see himself moving through the rooms.

Patrick looks at Rav's screen, tries to compose a sentence.

Bet you they don't like the changes, says Rav.

Yes, Patrick says. What on earth are you talking about? he thinks.

It could get sticky, says Rav. Heads could roll.

Patrick tries again. Anyway, he says. It's Friday.

Yeah. Can't wait. Antony's party tonight.

Ah, says Patrick. This is it, his opportunity. Do you think – is it too – does he need to know in advance?

Wouldn't have thought so, shrugs Rav. You got something on?

Then Patrick realises that the whole of their previous conversation will have passed through Rav's mind like a vapour.

Nothing important, he says.

Cool, says Rav.

I mean, I don't need to decide now – you think?

Rav looks at him for a second then back to the screen. It's open house, man. Just turn up.

I'll see.

But he feels a rush of relief. Rav invited me, he can say. If challenged. If Antony, opening the door, looks down on him, surprised. He can say it first thing, before Antony gets a chance to speak. Rav said it would be OK. Is it OK? And Antony will not be able to say no.

Then the clients arrive. Everyone is standing up, shaking hands, talking about trains and traffic and the weather. Looking at the clients, Patrick suddenly sees that Rav is right. They will hate the new section. He sits down, prepares to explain, yet again, why he cannot give them the stupid thing they want.

Patrick is about to go home when a meeting request slides onto his screen. It is from the account manager, the youngest yet, a Prince2 evangelist who has never seen a line of SQL. Patrick defers the meeting until Monday and leaves the office, eight hours and two minutes after he arrived.

He takes the bus home. The bus is full, people standing in the aisle, falling against each other at every traffic light. The girl next to him is talking to her phone. She wriggles and curls into it as she talks. Sometimes she chews her nail. Yeah, she says. Yeah. I know. Yeah. Isn't it the worst. Did you see what she said? I nearly died. It's just the worst thing ever.

He gets off the bus and walks through the side streets to his house. The pavements are lined with skips. Dust-sheets spill out over doorsteps. The builders are clearing up for the weekend, tipping out barrowloads of plaster. The houses here are always being built. The builders do them up and then three years later they come back and take them apart. They knock down the walls, tear out the kitchens, chisel up the tiles that they knelt over for two days, their backs still remember it. The builders are white with lime, their eyes are red. They watch Patrick pass with his clean shoes and clean fingernails. They narrow their eyes, sucking at a cigarette as if it has something to tell them.

Patrick unlocks his door and hangs his keys up on their hook. He goes to the kitchen and looks around. He adjusts the position of a mug. He turns a saucepan fractionally, so that the handles are all in line, at forty-five degrees to the shelf.

If anyone saw him they would think this was a symptom, OCD or GAD or an unnamed neurosis grown out of living alone for so long. But he knows it is just a habit. He will be able to stop it the moment he has reason to. The moment, for example, he is not living alone.

He opens the freezer. There will be something in there that he can eat, watching the news. He can always count on that.

After dinner, he shaves, thinking about the party, about the possibilities. He thinks how it will be to come home to someone else. He sees a shadowy figure watching his television, making coffee in his kitchen, hanging her silky clothes in his wardrobe. He will have to make room in his wardrobe.

He doesn't usually shave at this time, in this light. He notices grey hairs at his parting.

He should really be looking for another job. He has been in this one too long, it will look bad. And there are young people coming along all the time. New technologies. He sees the years of his working life plotted in employer-friendly segments, progressing in orderly sequence to the edge of the mirror.

His first job was at a finance company in London. He'd excelled at university, could have gone on, if he'd wanted, to postgraduate work, an academic position, but he never thought seriously about anything other than lining up his first proper job. The work was simple, a monkey could have done it. But the salary was pretty good for a college leaver, even one with a First and some work experience.

He shared the top floor of a narrow terrace in Balham with Roy, who'd been on his course in Manchester. Roy was quiet and studious, although not particularly bright. He'd been lucky to get his 2.1. After a short time they were joined by a French girl, Cecile, who, as far as Patrick could tell, was someone Roy had bumped into on the tube. They had never discussed adding a third flatmate, and Patrick had been surprised and a little put out to find her living with them.

Cecile was short and sturdy with wiry hair and very pale skin spattered with solid dark freckles, as if she'd held it over a flame. She was studying something unmarketably frivolous and working as an office cleaner and had no money at all. She had the smallest room, too small to let, a cupboard really, Patrick hadn't even noticed it was there when they first moved in. She slept on a futon on the floor, paid a fraction of the rent they did, and helped herself to their food. She was completely unembarrassed by this. But you know, I am poor, she would say. She spoke with little French puffs of air, as if she was trying to make her way through a room full of feathers. She took food from where she worked too, biscuits and fruit, yogurts that people had left in the fridge. They do not notice, she would say, and shrug. They have enough. She stole tea bags, presented them to Roy and Patrick. For you, she would say, as if it made up for all the rest. Me, I do not like tea even, puffing a feather aside.

He had never been sure quite how it happened. It was as if one night he'd thought about her differently, dreamt about her perhaps, and the next day things changed. There were odd conversations where she made false assumptions about him and didn't listen when he corrected them. There was giggling – hers – at things that weren't funny. And then some line was crossed. He saw her misused skin right up close. They had sex without speaking, as if it was something to be got through. Her body had corners, multiple limbs, they had difficulty fitting together. She was somewhat critical of his technique. None of this was unexpected, and he understood it would improve with time.

At weekends, when he went hiking, she came with him. But she seemed uncomfortable in the outside world. It was too bright, she said, too warm, too cold, too windy. She did not like to go uphill. Her shoes were never quite right, she didn't have the proper clothes, there were paths they could not go along because of mud or stones or undergrowth. Once they saw a deer and she screamed.

They went to places of interest, the Science Museum, the Natural History Museum, the Observatory. She was perfunctory among the exhibits, eager to reach the gift shop. There she would finger through every fridge magnet and mouse mat, every unfunctional plastic replica, until he would say Do you like that? and she would clasp her hands together and say Truly? Oh, thank you. She would take it home and add it to the collection of unfunctional plastic replicas on the narrow shelf above her futon. My memories, she would say. There was nothing there from before she had moved in, not even a photo of her family.

They went to the London Eye. She kept her hands over her face as they climbed above the city. On the South Bank, she worried about pickpockets. Although there was nothing in her pockets. When it rained, she would insist on returning to the tube. He would sit there, as they rushed through the darkness, looking at his drained reflection.

They began to stay in more, watch television with Roy, have their dinner in front of it. Patrick and Roy had got the television for the news, Roy's quiz shows. But Cecile liked soap operas. They watched *Emmerdale*, *EastEnders*, *Coronation Street*. They were not what Patrick had expected. The people were grim and unhappy, their faces exaggeratedly three-dimensional. They were mired in their tormented lives, beyond saving, sinking deeper with every twist and turn. Cecile took it very seriously. She would ask questions that Patrick barely understood. Roy, somehow, knew the answers, was able to fill her in on the years she had missed. She would listen to him wide-eyed. Patrick would leave them to it, take the plates to the kitchen, wash up, looking out at the bare, defeated strip of garden behind the house, the long rectangles of light from the downstairs flat shining across it, the occasional shadow of someone moving across the windows.

They did not share a bed. They had tried early on, but it had made her irritable. Increasingly, she got irritable whatever it was they tried to share. Meals, evenings out, the couch, most especially sex. Eventually it was easier just to give her everything, including, in the end, his room when he moved out, and possibly Roy, from whom he never heard again.

Patrick can still feel the relief he felt then, moving into his own place. The silence of it. For a long time he kept it empty, so that any noise echoed. Until it seemed the right thing to get a rug, a sofa, three cushions. Put up a photograph of the Peak District. He still has that photograph, it is hanging in the lounge, above the sealed-in space that used to be the hearth.

He puts on a clean shirt, clean jeans. Downstairs, he puts his wallet in his pocket, takes his key off the hook. He stands in the hall, looking at the key, thinking again of the changes to come. All he has to do is go. He turns the key over, keeps looking at it. A car goes down the street. He hears people walking past the front door, going out or coming home, laughing, joking.

Sometimes, late at night, he is woken from sleep by foxes in the patch of wasteland behind the house. The sound is one of terror, as if they are being torn limb from limb.

The room is dim. Coloured fabric has been draped over the lamps to soften their light. It reminds Patrick of parties at university, parties held by the cool people, with diaphanous scarves and candles. The sliding doors at the back of the room are open, the party spilling out into the garden, where fairylights have been strung over the trees and fences, reds and golds and silvers, like a remembered Christmas. Music is playing from another room, so that only the bass can be heard. It is the same music, it seems to Patrick, as he used to hear from his room at university.

Moving forward through the dusk, he looks around. It is true, they are here. Just like Rav said. In the dim swirling room, in the kitchen, on the terrace, in the garden. Pretty girls, tall girls, wild girls, kind girls.

His arrival is timely. They have been here long enough

for their gloss to melt. Their hair is mussed, their eyes are big and bruised. They have passed through the loud, energetic stage of drunkenness, and have become limp and sad. They are shaking their heads, covering their eyes, weeping. There is a girl sobbing in the corner by the window, and another lying on the lawn with her face in her arms, her shoulders heaving. At the back of the garden there are clusters of girls, nodding, murmuring, swinging their melancholy Polish hair.

As Patrick moves through the room and into the garden the girls look up. They turn, they sit up, they stop talking, they stop crying. They look at him with their blurred eyes. Their faces, tilted towards him, are water-colours splashed by rain. They wipe their tears away, the mascara soils their cheeks. They are tarnished, they are sorry, they are open. Hello, they whisper. They reach out to touch him as he passes. We're so glad you're here, they say. We're so glad you finally made it. The fairy-lights glint in their hair and on their wet faces, extend an unseasonable benevolent light over the garden and over the gardens beyond, where neighbours have come out to stand on tiptoe at their hedges, and as far as the road at the end of the gardens, where people walking by turn to see it, and their footsteps, almost unbidden, start to drift in that direction.

JONATHAN TRIGELL

Aperitifs With
Mr Hemingway

Dear Reader,

I've never been much of a reader myself. Except for the paper, *The Mail* mostly, not because I believe all that stuff, but it's an easy read. And there's some truth in it: a spell in the army would sort these kids out, that's for sure; teach them a bit of respect. No respect, that's what people say about young men today.

A couple of months ago, I was walking down the street – I'm still very mobile, really, for all my aches – when I saw these three youths, heads shaved like soldiers, but never been in the army, I can tell you that. They had to step aside for a pushchair and one of them shouts at the mother:

'I'll get out the way then, shall I? I'll shove that pram up your . . .' – a word I wouldn't even use in retelling, never mind on the street to a young mother – she was just a kiddie herself, really.

Nothing I could do, of course, except think how they

had no respect for a lady. And how different it all was in my day.

Anyway, like I say, I've never been big on books, but I always enjoyed Hemingway. He knew how to write without getting all blousy about it. Hemingway always got it spot on. I've read the lot, even that one which is more just like a guidebook to bullfighting than a story. I would have returned it, except, to be quite fair, it did more or less say so on the back. Besides, it was my Rose that bought it for me.

I always joked with Rose that I'd do a Hemingway if she went first. Joked, but quietly meant it too. Old Ernest, he ended it all with both barrels of a twelve-gauge. That's a decision, that's not a cry for help.

Only, things are always different in the event than in the mind. When poor old Rose died, I was too tired from all the nights sat slouch-backed beside her and there was too much to organise to think about myself. All I could think about was a lifetime of memories.

Rose, she wasn't sure about me, when she saw me again at the dance, on that leave home. We'd already started a sort of a correspondence, while I was in Korea. I'd asked a friend to remember me to her. We'd met once before, see, through that friend, at another dance. Only I couldn't really dance. Now they just sort of shake themselves around, but you had to know what to do back then. Me, I didn't know what to do, and my skin was thin and yellow like the paper of Korean lanterns, with long travel and just-shook malaria. And Rose, she wasn't sure.

We had a good time again, mind. Enough that I knew I had to make her mine. Enough that she agreed to meet me once more, on my next leave. We still wrote letters too, they kept me going, those words from Rose. Them and what I used to get up to with that little Army Nurse, Emily, some evenings. And my gun of course.

It gives a man a certain amount of pride having a gun. I used to be able to strip them and rebuild them in the dark. A gun can never be clean enough, can never be too well oiled. There is never time spent on looking after a gun which is time wasted. Some of these kids could do with knowing that, instead of wandering around with pistols tucked in their fancy underpants, swaggering so wide it looks like they've got their legs on back to front, talking giberdigook. I've seen them round the estate; they don't care if I see: people think you don't exist any more, when you get old. No respect.

Well, the next time I had leave, I was home for good. And first chance, I floated our Rose round the floor like I was Fred Astaire. She couldn't believe it, smiled and laughed like a loon.

Prim as a nun was that little Emily, but she couldn't half teach a fellow to dance. Well enough to win me my Rose anyhow, and that's all I ever wanted.

But after poor Rose passed, I had nothing again. All those happy years and then nothing. So I decided I'd get me a pistol. Something to look after, something to take a bit of pride in. And then, if I decided to do a Hemingway, I'd have it close to hand. I thought that would bring me a bit of comfort, knowing I was in control. There's dignity in that, there's grace in choosing your own time. There's no dignity in clinging on because Jesus suffered, so they want you to suffer too.

I had a fair idea where to start looking for a gun. Like I say, there's enough around this estate. No one took me too seriously at first, but they saw the look in my eyes and they saw the money. Your eyes don't age, not inside, and your money's still good.

The two that said they'd sell me one, they looked 22, 23, maybe a bit older, it gets hard to tell, they all look so young. They say you're getting old when the coppers start looking young. Even judges look young to me.

I dare say these two had seen a judge or two already. They wanted the money outright, but I said to show me the pistol first – I wasn't dug up yesterday – and the one showed me it. And it was beautiful – not beautiful like my Rose, but beautiful like a first car – a yank gun: a .38 revolver, Smith & Wesson, snub-nosed, nickel-plated, walnut-gripped. So I gave him the money right away then. But he wouldn't hand me over the gun.

'You'd only hurt yourself with this, granddad, now disappear.'

Well, of course I was only going to hurt myself: that was the whole point. But it's not for the likes of him to decide. A deal's a deal. They've got no respect, that's the problem. So I went forwards and just grabbed for it.

He was just stood there laughing, like he couldn't believe it. But I wasn't just a squaddy, I know some tricks; I done this disarming wrist-wrench on him. Came back to me like it was yesterday that old Fairbairn was showing us. Before you knew it, I had the gun and it was him trying to get it back off me.

Then his friend came at me as well. Gave me a dig in the ribs, right hard too. Nearly knocked me over.

So I shot him.

Calm as Christmas Eve, I tell you. Old Fairbairn might have been whispering in my ear: 'Move the revolver as if it's an extension of your arm; now squeeze the whole gun, don't jerk with your trigger finger; perfect.' And he was down. Straight down. No movement. No twitching. Not like that poor bloke I killed in Korea. No sound but the crack which still lingered in my good ear. Like a starting signal for something new, it was.

The other fella, he backed right away then. So I said to him:

'Why don't you just go on home, son? You can keep the money, I've never stolen a thing in my life, and I'm not gonna start now. You just go on home.'

And he's like 'Yes, sir, thank you, sir, three bags full, sir.' Just like it should be, if you ask me: a bit of respect for your elders. People say young men today have no respect. And maybe that's true. But you shoot their mate in the bloody face and they start listening all right.

I wended my way home too. A few police cars came past me, but they didn't stop. You get invisible eventually, you see. The older you get, the thinner your skin gets, until finally no one can see you at all any more.

Don't think I'll even use the gun now, not for a while. Funny, but it's given me a new lease of life: killing someone. Now I have to listen to all the regional news bulletins, buy every local paper. Gives me a bit of a purpose, somehow: seeing if I got away with it.

But I'm writing this, just in case I do make that decision. Just to explain it all a bit. Just out of respect, you might say.

If you're reading this now, then it means that I've gone for that drink with Mr Hemingway. But just a tipple, just to wet my whistle. Don't want to get unsteady; because after, I shall be dancing with my Rose.

NEIL CAMPBELL

Sun on Prospect Street

THEIR HOUSES ARE opposite a glue factory and they grow up knowing the smell of melting horses. Behind their houses the motorway runs in a constant raised drone, slicing through what once was a village. Parallel to the motorway, on the other side, is the canal that once carried limestone barges, parallel to that, the railway that still carries limestone.

By the side of the railway there is a football pitch with leaning over goalposts and a long line of trampled grass through the middle leading to mud in the penalty areas. Crows inspect the mud and complain about the noise from the motorway. The canal where balls are sometimes lost is floated on by ducks and geese and sometimes the diluted rainbows of fuel. The odd lone figure sits on the bank smoking and drinking lager by a long motionless rod dipped into the flat water. The other side of the canal bank is filled with rustling and cracking reeds. In the evening the branches of tall trees shadow a braided fringe across the water.

The canal leads under the arches of the motorway bridge, and they sit under it, at the precipice of a sloping concrete bank stained where water pours down it on rainy days and lessens the spray in the lanes above. Sometimes they graffiti the concrete canvas. One big painted swirl reads the legend *Baggers*. Smaller comments in marker pen surround it: *is a dick* being one. They eat crisps and drink cans of pop and wedge the cans and crisp packets in gaps in the concrete when they've finished. Above the reeds on the other side of the bank there is a field where a white horse drinks from a bathtub. When it rains the horse walks across the boggy field and stands under the motorway bridge. Geese float along the canal and under the bridge too, though ducks stay out among a million holes.

The summer holidays they waited so long for have becoming boring after only one week. Five more weeks seem to stretch out forever. They sit under the muted roar of the motorway. Joe flicks through the creased magazine that also curls up at either side from being rolled. He looks at the picture: a topless woman in a shower, foam covering her breasts. He looks through the rest of the magazine and passes it to Leo before asking, 'Have you got any pubes yet?'

Leo takes the magazine first then puts it down on the concrete by his side, where it curls up again. 'I'll have a look,' he says, holding out his tracksuit bottoms. 'Three. I've got three.'

'I've got more than that,' says Joe. Just then a man walks along the towpath below them at the bottom of the concrete slope. He is watching as his black dog threatens to jump in the canal after the ducks. Leo shouts, 'I've got three pubes!' and the man turns round and looks up to where they sit. Unimpressed, he walks on. Finally the dog plunges into the water and the ducks flap and crash away and the man has to drag his dog out, the fur all slick and heavy, dripping wet patterns on the path.

Joe looks at Leo and then at the magazine and Leo picks the magazine up and looks through it. Joe keeps looking down at the water. Sometimes a jogger passes along the path, then a man at the back of a barge. A sign painted on the wooden side of the barge spells *Desperado* and the man is wearing a cowboy hat. He sees them but avoids eye contact and instead stares out at the slow miles of canal ahead. A woman sits under a dark blue parasol at the other end of the barge. 'I'm going for my dinner,' says Joe, and Leo rolls up the magazine, stashes it behind a pillar and follows him down the back path to Prospect Street.

In the afternoon they go to the football pitch with Leo's ball. It's a Mitre casey they fished out of the canal the week before, when Leo fell in. The ball is white with little 'v' shapes all over it. They had to pump it up a bit with an adapter and a bicycle pump. If they kicked at goal from outside the area they would barely reach. And standing in the goal mouth Leo looks like he'll always be too tiny for a keeper. There's no netting in the goals so Leo has to run for the ball every time Joe scores and every time Joe hits it wide or over Joe has to go for it. After a while they play headers and volleys, Joe or Leo crossing from the side for one or the other to head or volley towards the empty goal. Both end up with mud on their heads. At one point Leo steps in some dog muck and spends an age wiping it off, twisting his ankle to slide his trainers on the grass. Joe is tired and so goes over and leans against a goal post, then sits down against it and wipes the sweat from his head, covering his hand with the dried mud off it. There's mud all over his trainers and on the inside right leg of his tracksuit bottoms. The afternoon sun is shining warm across the football pitch, glints on the canal and dazzles on vehicles whistling past on the motorway. It sinks across the chimneys of the terraced houses colouring the bricks red rose.

Leo wanders over, kicking the ball. 'There's none on the ball, is there?' asks Joe.

'No.'

'What about on your trainers?'

'No, look,' he says, lifting up his leg and turning the underside of his shoe so Joe can see.

Leo sits down on the ball next to Joe. A crow lands in the mud in the opposite goalmouth and pecks at the ground before leaning back to croak at them.

'When are you moving?' asks Leo.

'Next week, I think.'

There's a row of big houses along the main road into town. The houses back onto a railway line then reservoirs. Starting at one end they dart across lawns, duck under washing lines, scamper across patios, leave footsteps in flowerbeds, wobble over creosoted fences, send cats running, dogs barking and are pursued all the way by their shadows running sideways on the ground. At the end of the row they run over the railway lines and up onto the reservoirs, where the water shines vast and silver and spreads out before them as they climb the bank and look over the low stone wall.

'Do you think we could swim across there?' asks Leo.

'Don't be daft. We'd probably drown,' answers Joe.

'It's not that far.'

'Well I'm not doing it. What time do you have to be in?'

Leo looked at his watch. 'Oh shit, I'm too late already.'

Joe takes another look at the water, the ripples in the light wind a moving corrugation in the moonlight. They run down the grassy slope beside the stone steps, climb back over the wall again and follow the old farm track back to the road where the chevrons are lit by the orange of the streetlights and cars sometimes pass. A couple walk back from the pub, the woman's legs more wobbly than the man's so that she clings to his arm for support as well as love. On the distant motorway, lorries and cars and sometimes motorbikes flash past.

In the morning Leo comes running down the street rebounding the football off walls, bang bang bang, and crashing it into rattling metal gates, dribbling around cars, sometimes doing one-twos off their tyres, sending cats running out from under those cars and hackles rising over breakfasts.

Leo calls for Joe, climbing over the fence at the back, walking through the garden and knocking on the back door. Joe shouts him to come in and when he's finished his bowl of cereals Joe gets up and walks in his socks to the back door where he picks up his muddy trainers, puts them on and then takes the ball off Leo.

They walk together to the railway bridge and look through the metal grate at the straight lines stretching out as far as the brick bridge over the main road. The sunlight shines on the lines outside the tunnel and shows its curve to the left. Goldfinches flash over embankment brambles. Turning around and looking through the metal grate of the bridge in the other direction, they see the straight lines running to another brick bridge, where a lad called Wayne had fallen off and ended up in a wheelchair. From the elevation of the railway bridge they can see the canal and the motorway and the railway line, and the row of houses where they'd been garden creeping and beyond that the walls around the reservoir. They can smell the boiling bones in the glue factory. The fields across the bridge seem to stretch out for miles and they can see the distant hills in the summer sunlight. The fields are empty save for crows and one man walking a brown greyhound. Joe throws the football off the end of the metal bridge and onto the field and they run down the wooden steps after it. 'Bagsy not in net!' shouts Joe and Leo reluctantly kicks the ball to Joe and makes his way between the posts, where he stays until Joe hits one wide and they have to change around because that's the rule.

After they've been playing a while they can hear a distant cracking noise and something that seems to whistle in the grass beside them. It is only when Leo gets hit in the leg that they realise that someone is shooting pellets at them with an air gun. Then three lads are standing by the goalposts and watching.

'How's your leg?' one of them says to Leo, before giggling and not listening for an answer. Leo sits in the grass, rubbing the little red bump on his shin.

The three lads are all taller and the tallest of them starts punching Leo on the arm. Leo backs away and looks down at the floor and seems like he wants to cry. None of the lads approach Joe and he watches as it unfolds. Leo doesn't fight back and so eventually all three of the taller lads are punching him on the arms and kicking him in the shins. Leo stands there and takes it and Joe watches, and then eventually one of the taller lads punches Leo in the face and Leo finally starts crying and the three taller lads run off laughing across the fields.

Leo sits on the grass wiping his eyes and then returns to rubbing his leg where the pellet hit. His face is all red from crying. Joe stands over the football looking at him.

'What are you looking at?' says Leo.

'Nothing,' says Joe. 'Who were they?' he asks, but Leo doesn't answer or even look up from the shin he is rubbing.

'I want my ball back,' says Leo.

'It's not yours,' says Joe, and kicks it in his direction before walking towards home over the railway bridge. On the bridge he stops and looks back and Leo is just gazing down at the grass and not moving.

The next week Joe watches from his bedroom window as a removal man helps Leo's mum and dad put furniture into a big white van. Leo comes out carrying a duvet and a bedside lamp. The van blocks the road and a car that wants to get through is stopped and has to turn around and go back the other way. It takes them a long time to load up the van. Eventually Joe sees the white van pull away, Leo and his parents following in the car behind. He looks at the back of Leo's head until the car turns right at the end of Prospect Street.

The Room Beyond

A S SOON AS Todd drove off the motorway it vanished from the mirror, and so did the sun across the
moor. On both sides of the street the slender terraced
houses huddled together like old folk afraid of descend-
ing the precipitous slope. Most of the shops in the town
at the foot of the street were illuminated, but the streetlamps seemed oblivious of the September dusk. As he
braked and braked again he saw the hotel sign across the
maze of roofs.

The middle was blocked by the spire of a church, but
BEL and the final E were visible. He hadn't realised that
the hotel was on the far side of town. Whenever he stayed
with his uncle and aunt he'd come by train, from which
they had escorted him through the back streets to their
house, interrogating him and talking at him so incessantly
that he'd had little chance to learn the route. It had been
the same on Sundays, when they'd walked to the Bellevue for a dauntingly formal lunch. Now the town hardly
seemed large enough to accommodate either route.

More than this had changed in fifty years. While the
clock from beneath which figures emerged on the hour
was still outside the jewellers on the High Street, the road
was one way only now. It turned away from the hotel,

and all the side streets leading there displayed No Entry signs. Most of the shops were either new or disused, and the Apollo, where he'd once seen an airman climbing steps to heaven, had become the Valley Bottom pub. In a few minutes Todd found himself back at the clock, which hadn't moved on from twenty-five to six. The tarnished figures were paralysed on their track, and one stood in a miniature doorway as if he were loath to venture beyond. Shops were being shuttered, and at last the streetlamps came on, illuminating virtually deserted streets. This time Todd left the High Street ahead of the bend, but the lane he followed returned to the clock. He glimpsed Christ the Redeemer down a narrow alley, though the church was dark. He had to drive along the High Street yet again to discover that a road around the outside of the town led towards the hotel.

Was the park beside the road the one where his relatives had taken him to hear a brass band? He wouldn't have placed it so close to the hotel. The doctor's surgery must have been in one of the derelict houses facing the park, but Todd couldn't identify which. He hadn't thought of it for all these years, and he would have been happy to forget it now. He hadn't passed a single inhabited house by the time the road brought him to the hotel.

He had to laugh, as his uncle liked him to. The long black building was less than half the size he seemed to remember. While it might have been designed to resemble a mansion, he could have taken it for some kind of institution now. A wind blundered off the moor and flapped a torn section of the canvas awning across most of the unilluminated name. A couple of cars were parked on the forecourt, under a solitary orange floodlight that turned his blue Passat as black as they appeared to be. Dead windblown vegetation splintered beneath the wheels as he parked in front of a tall window blacked out by heavy curtains. His boxy suitcase was resting on the back seat, and he trundled it to the hotel.

No uniformed doorman was waiting to sweep the massive glass door wide, and Todd might have imagined that the door itself had shrunk. Its metal corner scraped over the tiled floor with an excruciating screech that made the receptionist glower. She was a brawny broad-shouldered woman with gilded spectacles as narrow as her eyes. Her grey hair was severely waved, and the glasses seemed to pinch her features small and sharp. She kept up her frown as Todd crossed the lobby, which was lit to some extent by a few bulbs of the dusty chandelier. More than just her attitude reminded him of someone else, so that he blurted 'Excuse me, did you have a mother?'

She pursed her lips so hard that the surrounding skin turned grey along with them. 'I beg your pardon,' she said while doing nothing of the kind.

Her voice was hoarse and blurred, like a smoker's who was also somewhat drunk. 'Sorry,' Todd said and risked a laugh, only to wish he'd kept it to himself. 'Does it run in the family, I meant to say.'

'I'm sure I don't know what you mean.'

'What you do. Admitting. Admission.' Todd's words seemed to be straying out of his control, an unwelcome reminder of his age. 'What I'm trying to say,' he said, 'was she a receptionist? The one in the practice by the park round the corner.'

'That's a graveyard, not a park.'

He could only assume she had somewhere else in mind. 'Anyway,' he said, 'can I have my room?'

'Have you booked?'

'I rang,' Todd said and wondered if the woman who'd

taken the call had been her in a more hospitable mood. 'Jacob Todd.'

'Todd.' His uncle used to greet him with a cry of 'Now it's all jake,' but Todd felt as if the receptionist had dropped his name with a dull thud. She dragged a ledger bound in black from under the counter and plucked at the pages before repeating 'Todd' like an accusation. He might have thought the pages at the back were loose with age until he realised they were registration forms, one of which she laid before him on the counter. 'Fill yourself in,' she said.

Discolouration had lent the form a dark border. The print was both small and smudged, and squinting at it only left Todd more frustrated with the task it set him. 'Who needs all this?'

The receptionist raised her spectacles to train her gaze on him. Her fingertips looked as earthy as the edges of the form. 'You might be taken ill,' she said.

'Suppose I am, who'll want all this information?'

'The authorities,' she said and stared unblinkingly at him.

The solitary writing instrument on the counter was a ballpoint splintered like a bone and bandaged with sticky plastic tape. As Todd strove to fit his details into narrow boxes on the form, the inky tip stumbled about like a senile limb. Last name, first name, address, date of birth, place of birth . . . 'What's your business in our town?' the receptionist said.

'A funeral.'

'You'll be just round the corner.'

Even if that was indeed a graveyard, it needn't be the only one in town. Christ the Redeemer hadn't appeared to be anywhere near the hotel. Todd could go for a walk and find his way to the church once he'd checked into his room. Profession, driving licence number, car registration number, telephone number, email . . . 'Will you be taking the dinner?' the receptionist said.

Todd was distracted by someone's attempts to enter the hotel or even to locate the handle of the door. He turned to see that the door was shaking just with rain, which was surging across the moor. 'When do you need to know?' he said.

'As soon as you like.' This plainly meant as soon as she did. 'Cook wants to get away.'

Perhaps at least the meal would be up to the standard Todd remembered, and he could save his walk in case the rain ceased. 'Put me down, then,' he said.

The receptionist vanished like a shadow into a small office behind the counter. Presumably the dim light from the lobby was all she required, for Todd heard the rattle of a telephone receiver. 'One for dinner,' she said, and somewhere in the building a distant version of her voice joined in. Another hollow rattle was succeeded by a metallic one, and she reappeared with a key attached to a tarnished baton. 'Are you written up yet?' she said.

Towards the bottom of the form the print was almost too indistinct to read. Method of payment, onward destination, next of kin . . . 'That's a blank, I'm afraid,' Todd said. He scrawled his signature, in which age had reduced the first name to resembling Jab, and unstuck his discoloured fingers from the pen while the receptionist pored over the form.

He'd had more than enough of the sight of her greyish scalp through her irregular parting – it put him in mind of a crack in weedy stone – by the time she raised her head. 'Retired from what?' she apparently felt entitled to learn.

'Education.' When this didn't lessen her scrutiny Todd added 'Teaching them their sums.'

This failed to earn him even a blink. 'Will you be dressing?' she said.

'For dinner, you mean?' She'd begun to remind him of his aunt, who had always found some element of his appearance to improve – a collar to tug higher on his neck, a tie to yank tighter, a handkerchief that was either lying too low in his breast pocket or standing too impolitely erect. 'I'll be changing,' he said.

'Better look alive, then. It's nearly eight, you know.'

'Nowhere near,' said Todd, shaking the cuff of his heavy sweater back from his thin wrist. He was about to brandish the time – not much after half past five – when he saw his watch had stopped. His aunt and uncle had sent it for his twenty-first, and it had never let him down before. He drew his cuff over its battered face and found the receptionist frowning at him as if he'd betrayed some innumeracy. 'Let's have my key, then,' he said, 'and I'll be down as soon as I'm fit to kill.'

Whenever she'd finished sprucing him Todd's aunt used to say that was how he was dressed, but perhaps the receptionist didn't know the phrase. 'You're number one,' she informed him, planting the brass club on the counter with a blow like the stroke of a hammer. 'You'll have to work the lift yourself.'

Todd couldn't tell whether she was apologising for the attendant's absence or reminiscing about the hotel's better days. As he headed for the gloomy alcove that housed the entrance to the single lift, a wheel of his suitcase dislodged a loose tile. The receptionist watched with disfavour while he replaced it in its gritty niche, and he didn't linger over deciphering the blurred letters on the underside of the tile – presumably some firm's trademark. Once he dragged open both latticed doors of the lift he struggled over shutting them. The wall of the lift shaft inched past the rusty mesh, and at last the floor of a grudgingly illuminated corridor sank into view, although the lift fell short of aligning with it. Todd had to clamber up and haul his suitcase after him before he could make for his room.

It was at the far end of the left-hand stretch of corridor, where a window above a fire escape showed the town reduced to runny mud by the rain on the glass. The feeble lamps on the corridor walls resembled glazed flames, all the more by flickering. The number on Todd's door was dangling head down from its one remaining screw. He twisted the key in the aged shaky lock and pushed the leaden door open, to be met by a smell of old fabric. It made Todd feel enclosed, invisibly and impalpably but oppressively, even after he switched on the miniature chandelier.

The small room was darkened by the furniture – a black wardrobe with a full-length mirror in its narrow door, an ebony dressing-table, a squat chest of drawers that looked stunted by age, a bed that wasn't quite single or double, with a hint of an indentation underneath a shaggy blanket as brown as turned earth. A door led to a shower and toilet, while another would have communicated with the next bedroom but was blocked by a luggage stand. Behind the heavy curtains at the foot of the bed Todd found a window that showed him darkness raging above the moor. He was unpacking his case when he heard what could have been the fall of several pans in the kitchen. As he changed into his dark suit – the only one he'd brought – a phone rang.

At first he thought it was in the next room. It shrilled at least a dozen times before he traced the dusty wire from the skirting board to the upper compartment of the wardrobe. When he swung the door open, the receiver toppled off the hook, starting to speak as he fumbled it towards his face. 'The gong's gone, Mr Todd.'

The receptionist's tone seemed capable of stripping Todd of all the years since his last visit. 'Oh, is that what it was?' he retorted. 'I'll be with you as soon as I can.'

He would have liked to shower and shave, but the hotel could take the blame, even if the man in the black frame of the mirror would never have passed his aunt's inspection. Todd had always felt on probation, never quite knowing if his visits were treats or punishments. 'If you won't behave you can go to your aunt's,' his mother used to say, and he'd suspected she was a little afraid of her older sister. His uncle hadn't seemed to be, and made a joke wherever he could find one, but then he'd done so at the surgery as well. Todd didn't need to be alone with those memories, and hurried out of the room.

If he'd been able to locate the stairs he would have used them, but the corridor offered him just the silent doors, bearing numbers like steps in a child's first arithmetic lesson. He was close to hearing them chanted in his skull. He stepped gingerly down into the lift and pushed the marble button, only to leave a blotchy print on it. He hadn't even washed his hands. 'Not my fault,' he muttered, feeling threatened by a second childhood.

The lobby was deserted except for a sign on a stand outside a room Todd hadn't previously noticed. The plastic numbers separated by a hyphen weren't years, they were hours with just sixty minutes between them. The words above them would have said DINING ROOM if they hadn't lost a letter. Todd found the N on the carpet in the doorway – carpet trampled as flat and black as soil. As he attempted to replace the letter between the I and its twin he felt as if he were playing an infantile game. He hadn't succeeded when he grew aware of being watched from the room beyond the sign. 'Just putting you together,' he said.

The waiter was dressed even more sombrely than Todd. He stepped back a silent pace and indicated the room with a sweep of one white-gloved hand. The room was nowhere near as daunting as Todd recalled. While the tables were still draped like altars, and the place was certainly as hushed as a church, it was scarcely big enough for a chapel. Even if it had always sported chandeliers, he didn't remember them as being so ineffectual. He had to squint to be sure of the burly waiter's small sharp face, the eyes narrowed as though in need of spectacles, the brow that he could have imagined had been tugged unnaturally smooth by the removal of a wig from the clipped grey hair. He was disconcerted enough to blurt 'Has your sister gone off?'

The waiter paced to the farthest table and drew back its solitary chair. 'Who was that, sir?'

His voice was as unctuously slow as a priest's at a pulpit, and might have been striving for hoarseness and depth. 'Aren't you related to the lady at reception?' Todd said.

'They say we're all related, don't they?' Before Todd could give this whatever response it deserved, the waiter said 'Will you be taking the buffet?'

Todd sat down as the waiter slipped the chilly leather seat beneath him. 'Can I see the menu?' he said.

He never had while he was visiting – he'd only watched his aunt and uncle leafing through leather-bound volumes and then ordering for him. 'I wouldn't recommend it, sir,' the waiter said.

Todd was starting to feel as he'd felt as a child – that everyone around him knew a secret he wouldn't learn until he was older. 'Why not?' he demanded.

'We're just providing the buffet option on this occasion. Chef had to leave us.'

'Then I haven't much choice, have I?'

'We always have while we're alive.'

The waiter sounded more priestly than ever, and his pace was deliberate enough for a ritual as he approached the lengthy table that stood along the left side of the room. He uncovered every salver and tureen before extending a hand towards them. 'Enough for a large party, sir.'

When waiters used to say things like that, Todd had expected his uncle to respond with a witticism. The hotel seemed to be turning into a joke Todd didn't understand. As he crossed the shiny blackened carpet to the buffet, the waiter raised a cloth from an elongated heap at the end of the table and handed him a plate. The buffet offered chicken legs and slices of cold meat, potatoes above which a fog hovered or at least a stagnant cloud of steam, a mound of chips that reminded him of extracting sticks from a haphazard pile in a game for which his aunt had never had the patience. Last came salads, and as he loaded his plate a lettuce leaf attempted a feeble crawl before subsiding on the salver. The movement might have betrayed the presence of an insect, but it was the work of a wind that had moved the floor-length curtain away from a window behind the table as though somebody was lurking there. As a child Todd had somehow been led to believe that God lived behind the curtains above the altar in the church. The curtains on the far side of the table veiled only a vast darkness tossing restlessly as a sleeper in a nightmare. He did his best to ignore the impression while remarking 'At least I'm the first one down.'

'The only one,' the waiter said and found utensils under the cloth for him. 'It's all been put on for you, Mr Todd.'

Was this meant to shame him into taking more? Todd

might have wondered if his fellow guests knew better than to eat at the hotel, but he was more inclined to ask how the waiter knew his name. The man spoke before Todd could. 'Will you be having the house?'

'I'll try a bottle. Make it red.' In a further attempt to recapture some sense of maintaining control Todd said 'And a jug out of the tap.'

The waiter gave a priestly bow before gliding through a doorway to the left of the buffet, and Todd heard him droning to himself under his breath. Any response was in the same voice, and monotonous enough to suggest that the man was murmuring a ritual. After some sounds of pouring the waiter reappeared with a tray that bore an unstoppered carafe and a jug. He served Todd water and wine and stepped back. 'Can you taste it, sir?' he murmured.

Todd took a mouthful of the wine, which seemed oddly lifeless, like some kind of token drink. 'It'll do,' he said, if only to make the waiter step back.

The man continued loitering within rather less than arm's length. He'd clasped his hands together on his chest, which put Todd in mind of someone praying beside a bed. When he tried to concentrate on his meal the hands glimmered so much at the edge of his vision that he might have imagined the gloves were plastic. 'I'll be fine now,' he said as persuasively as he could.

The waiter seemed reluctant to part his hands or otherwise move. At last he retreated, so slowly that he might have felt he didn't exist apart from his job. 'Call me if there's anything you need,' he said as he replaced the covers on the buffet before withdrawing into the inner room. He began murmuring again at once, which made it hard for Todd to breathe. It reminded him too much

of the voice he used to hear beyond the doctor's waiting-
room.

'Go to the doctor's with your uncle,' his aunt would
say, and Todd had never known whether she disliked
having him in the house by herself or was providing her
husband with company if not distraction, unless it had
been her way of making certain that Todd's uncle saw the
doctor yet again. Every time he'd filled the wait with jokes
at which Todd had felt bound to laugh, although neither
the quips nor his mirth had seemed to please the other
patients. He'd felt not just embarrassed but increasingly
aware that the joking was designed to distract someone –
himself or his uncle or both – from the reason they were
waiting in the room. He had never ventured to ask, and
his uncle hadn't volunteered the information. It had been
the secret waiting beyond the door through which his
uncle would disappear with a last wry grin at Todd, after
which Todd would gaze at the scuffed carpet while he
tried to hear the discussion muffled by the wall. Eventually
his uncle would return, looking as if he'd never given up
his grin. While Todd had seldom managed to distinguish
even a word, he'd once overheard his uncle protest 'This
isn't much of a joke.'

Todd knew the secret now, but he preferred not to
remember. He was even glad to be distracted by the
waiter, who had stolen at some point back into the dining-room. Todd seemed to have been so preoccupied
that he might have imagined somebody else had eaten
his dinner, which he couldn't recall tasting. The jug and
carafe were empty too. He'd barely glanced at his plate
when the waiter came swiftly but noiselessly to him. 'Do
go back, Mr Todd.'

The subdued light and the oppressive silence, not to
mention the buffet, were making Todd feel as if he were

already at a wake. 'I've finished, thank you,' he said. 'The doctor says I have to watch my food.'

When his uncle used to say that, Todd could never tell if it was a joke. Certainly his uncle had gazed at his food until his wife protested 'Don't put ideas in the boy's head, Jack.' Since the waiter seemed ready to persist, Todd said 'I'll be down in the morning. I have to be ready for a funeral.'

The waiter looked lugubriously sympathetic, but Todd was thrown by the notion that the man already had. 'Whose is that, sir?'

'I'd rather not talk about it if you don't mind.' Todd regretted having brought the subject up. 'I'm on my own now,' he said as he made his way between the empty tables, which had begun to remind him of furniture covered with dustsheets in an unoccupied house. When he glanced back from the lobby the waiter was nowhere to be seen, and Todd's place was so thoroughly cleared that he might never have been there. A curtain stirred beside the long uneven mound draped from head to foot on the buffet table, and Todd discovered he would rather not see the mound stir too. He made some haste to leave before he realised that he didn't know when breakfast was served. Calling 'Hello?' brought him no response, neither from the dining-room nor from the impenetrably dark office beyond the reception counter. He'd arrange to be wakened once he was in his room.

Why did he expect to be met in the lift? He was close to fancying there was no room for anyone but him as soon as he returned to the panelled box. He fumbled the gates shut and watched the wall ooze past them like a mudslide. He was anxious for light to appear above it well before that happened, and as soon as the lift wobbled to a halt he clambered up into the corridor.

It was as silent as ever. The sombre doors between the dim glazed flames could easily have reminded him of a mausoleum. The rain on the window at the end was borrowing colours from the lights of the town. The storm was slackening, and Todd was able to read some of the illuminated signs. Beneath the race of headlamps on the motorway he made out several letters perched on a high roof – ELLE and also U. An unwelcome thought took him to the window, on which he couldn't distinguish his breath from the unravelling skeins of rain. The sign swam into focus as if he were regaining his vision, and he saw it belonged to the Bellevue Hotel.

If anybody heard his gasp of disbelief, they gave no response. For a moment he had no idea where he was going, and then he found his numbered baton and jammed the key into the lock. A few bulbs flared in the dwarfish chandelier – not as many as last time, but they showed him the shabby leather folder on the dressing-table. He threw the folder open on the bed, revealing a few dog-eared sheets of notepaper and a solitary envelope. While he couldn't tell how much of their brownishness the items owed to age, there was no mistaking the name they bore. He was in the Belgrave Hotel.

It might have been yet another element of a joke that somebody was playing on him, unless he was playing it on himself. He was too late to change hotels, whatever time it was – 'too late, Kate,' as his uncle liked to say even when Todd's aunt wasn't there. Just now Todd wanted nothing more than to lie down, but first he needed to arrange his morning call.

He retrieved the phone from the upper cupboard of the wardrobe, only to find no instructions on the yellowed paper disc in the middle of the dial. When he picked up the bony receiver he heard a sound not unlike a protracted breathless gust of wind, presumably the Belgrave's version of a dialling tone. 9 seemed the likeliest number, but when he tried it Todd heard a phone begin to ring along the corridor. He was tempted to speak to his fellow guest, if only to establish there was one, but the hollow muffled note tolled until he cut it off. Dialling 1 brought him only the empty tone, and so he tried the zero. A bell went off in the depths of the building and was silenced, and a slow hoarse blurred voice in his ear said 'Mr Todd.'

'Can you get me up for eight?'

'For how many would that be, sir?'

'I'm saying can you see I'm down for breakfast. What time's that?'

'Eight will do it, Mr Todd.'

Had the receptionist heard his first question after all? Todd was too weary to say any more – almost too exhausted to stand up. He stumbled to the token bathroom, where he lingered as briefly as seemed polite. The shower cubicle put him in mind of a cramped lift that had somehow acquired plumbing, while the space outside it was so confined it almost forced the toilet under the sink. Another reason for him to leave the windowless room was the mirror, but the wardrobe door showed him more of the same, displaying how age had shrunken and sharpened his face. He switched off the light and clambered into bed.

The indentation in the mattress made it easiest for him to lie on his back, hands crossed on his breastbone. He heard a hollow plop of rain on wood and then an increasingly sluggish repetition of the sound, which put him in mind of heartbeats. The wind was more constant, keeping up an empty drone not unlike the voiceless noise of the receiver. Though he'd remembered one of his uncle's favourite turns of phrase – the comment about lateness

– it didn't revive as many jokes as Todd hoped. It only brought back his uncle's response to hearing the doctor's receptionist call his name. 'That's me,' he would say, 'on my tod.'

It wasn't even true. His nephew had been with him, sharing the apprehension the man had been anxious if not desperate to conceal. None of these were memories Todd wanted to keep close to him in the dark. With an effort he recalled names his uncle had dug up from history: Addled Hitler, Guiser Wilhelm, Josef Starling, Linoleum Bonypart, Winsome Churchill . . . For years Todd had believed they had all been alive at the same time. Now the names seemed more like evidence of senility than jokes – blurred versions of the past that put him in mind of the way the rain on the window had twisted the world into a different shape. They left him unsure of himself, so that he was grateful to hear a voice.

It was next door. No, it was beyond the other room, though not far, and apparently calling a name. Presumably the caller wanted to be let in, since Todd heard a door open and shut. For a while there was silence, and then someone came out of the adjoining bathroom – a door opened, at any rate. As Todd tried to use the hint of companionship to help him fall asleep, he grew aware of more sounds in the next room.

His neighbour must be drunk. They seemed to be doing their utmost to speak – to judge by their tone, striving to voice some form of protest – but so unsuccessfully that Todd might have imagined they had no means of pronouncing words. He was struggling to make sense of it, since it was impossible to ignore, when someone else spoke. Was it the voice he'd first heard? Or perhaps the guest in the next room but one was calling for quiet. In a moment a door opened and closed. Todd willed the silence to let him sleep, but he was still awake when he heard the door again, followed by activity in the other room. His neighbour seemed to be in a worse state than ever, and had given up any attempt to speak while bumping into all the furniture. After some time the ungainly antics subsided, letting Todd hope his neighbour had found the bed or at least fallen asleep. But a voice was calling a name, and the door was audible again. By now Todd knew the silence wouldn't last, and he reared up from the trough of the mattress. 'What are you doing in there?' he shouted.

The darkness engulfed his protest as somebody came back into the next room. They no longer sounded able to walk. They were crawling about on the floor, so effortfully that Todd fancied he heard them thumping it with their hands if not clawing at it. He'd had enough, and he lurched off the bed, groping at the dark until he found the light-switch. As soon as a couple of bulbs flickered in the chandelier he stumbled along the corridor to knock on the door of his neighbour's room.

The huge indifferent voice of the dark answered him – the wind. He pounded on the door until the number shivered on its loose screw, but nobody responded. The nearest glazed flame lent the digit a vague shadow that came close to transforming it into an 8, although Todd was reminded of a different symbol. It would have needed to be lying down, as he did. He thumped on the door again as a preamble to tramping back to his room. He parted his thin dry lips as he snatched the receiver off the hook and heard its empty sound. It was the wind, and the instrument was dead as a bone.

As he let the receiver drop into its cradle he heard the door in the next room. He couldn't take a breath while he listened to the noises that ensued. His neighbour was crawling about as blindly as before but less accurately than ever. It took them a considerable time to progress across the room. Todd would have preferred them not to find the connecting door, especially once he heard a fumbling at the bottom of it, a rudimentary attempt that sounded too undefined to involve fingers. As the door began to shake, a rage indistinguishable from panic swept away Todd's thoughts. Grabbing the suitcase, he flung it on the bed and dragged the luggage stand aside. He heard a series of confused noises in the other room, as if somebody were floundering across it, retreating in an agony of embarrassment at their own state. The connecting door wasn't locked, and he threw it wide open.

The next room was deserted, and it wasn't a bedroom. By the light from his own room Todd made out two low tables strewn with open books and magazines. Against the walls stood various chairs so decrepit that they seemed to need the dimness to lend them more substance. If the room hadn't been deserted he might not have ventured in, but he felt compelled to examine the items on the tables, like a child determined to learn a secret. He was halfway across the stained damp carpet when he wished he hadn't left his room.

The books were textbooks, in so many pieces that they might have been dismantled by someone's fumbling attempts to read them. There were no magazines, just scattered pages of the oversized books. Despite the dimness, Todd was able to discern more about the illustrations than he even slightly liked. All of them depicted surgical procedures he wanted to believe could never have been put into practice, certainly not on anyone alive or still living afterwards. Mixed up with the pages were sheets of blank paper on which someone had drawn with a ballpoint pen, perhaps the taped-up pen that lay among them. Its unsteadiness might explain the grotesque nature of the drawings, which looked like a child's work or that of someone unusually crippled. In a way Todd was grateful that he couldn't judge whether the drawings were attempts to reproduce the illustrations from the textbooks or to portray something even worse. He was struggling to breathe and to retreat from the sight of all the images, not to mention everything they conjured up, when he heard the door shut behind him.

He whirled around to find he could still see it – could see it had no handle on this side. He only had to push it open, or would have except that it was locked. He was throwing all his weight against it, the very little weight he seemed to have left, when a voice at his back said 'Mr Todd.'

It was the voice he'd been hearing, as hoarse and practically as blurred as it had sounded through the wall. 'You don't want me,' he pleaded, 'you want someone else,' but the silence was so eloquent that he had to turn. He still had one hope – that he could flee into the corridor – but the door to it had no handle either. The only open door was on the far side of the room.

The doorway was admitting the light, such as it was. When he trudged across the waiting-room he saw that the source of the dim glow was a solitary bare bulb on a tattered flex. It illuminated a room as cramped as a trench. The bare rough walls were the colour of earth, which might be the material of the floor. The room was empty apart from a long unlidded box. Surely the box might already contain someone, and Todd ventured forward to see. He had barely crossed the threshold when a voice behind him murmured 'He's gone at last.' They switched off the power and shut him in, and the light left him so immediately that he had no time to be sure that the room was another antechamber.

WILL SELF

iAnna

D R SHIVA MUKTI, a psychiatrist at St Mungo's, a small and down-at-heel general hospital situated – rather bizarrely – in the dusty pit left behind when the Middlesex Hospital was demolished in the spring of 2008, had, through various serpentine manipulations, got hold of his senior colleague Dr Zack Busner's mobile phone number, and this he proceeded to call: 'Who is it?' Busner snapped. He was lying naked on his bed in the bedroom of the grotty first-floor flat he had recently rented on Fortess Road in Kentish Town above an insurance broker's. His phone had been balanced on the apex of his sweat-slicked tumulus of a belly, and when it rang it slid down, slaloming expertly through his cleavage, bounced off his clavicle and hit him full in his froggy mouth. Mukti identified himself and explained why he was calling. Busner responded disjointedly: 'Yes . . . oh, yes . . . Yes, I remember you – no, no I'm not. No – I'm not inter- For heaven's sake man, I'm *retired*, I don't want to examine your patient no matter how novel her symptoms may be . . . What's that? Not the first, you say – something of an emerging pattern . . . ?'

It was too late – the older psychiatrist had allowed himself to be hooked. Rocking then rolling off the bed he stood with the phone caught in the corner of his mouth. Then the call pulled him into his clothes, out the door, down the stairs (through the wall he heard things like: 'Third party in Chesham, John?' and 'Better try Aviva . . .'), out the front door, down the road to the tube, down the escalator, through the grimy piping and up another escalator, until he found himself, landed and gasping below a flaking stucco portico beside a billboard picturing computer-generated luxury flats, 1,800 of them.

Mukti was a tannish, goatishly good-looking man in his late thirties with thick blue-black hair that grew low on a brow contorted with furious concentration. He pointed to the small window set in the door of the treatment room and said: 'She's in there.' Busner peered though. A young schizophrenic woman wearing a middle-aged charity shop twinset sat erect on a plastic chair making fluidly elegant motions with her skinny arms. She poked the space in front of her, tweaking and tweezering it with her quick-bitten fingers as if it were a semi-resistant medium. Busner was reminded of the 1970s and Marcel Marceau. 'She thinks the world is an iPad,' Mukti explained.

'An I-what?' Busner was nonplussed.

'An iPad – a sort of computer you operate by touching the images on its screen. If you observe closely you'll see that she's pointing to objects in the room – the examina-tion couch, a lamp, a sharps bin – then instead of focussing on them directly, she parts her fingers and this increases the size of the image for her.'

'Can we go in?' Busner asked.

'Certainly,' Mukti couldn't help sounding smug, 'but I've discovered the best way of interacting with her is to go with the flow of her iPad world . . . If we wait a moment she'll notice us on her screen, then point and enlarge us, after that she'll experience our presence as video clip.

They slipped into the corner of the treatment room and presently the young woman did indeed enlarge the two shrinks. Ignoring them, she continued talking to an invisible interlocutor in a brittle self-conscious voice, saying things such as, 'Well, they would, wouldn't they' and 'No, I saw him last night but he was going to the Hope and Anchor . . .' Busner whispered to Mukti: 'I assume she thinks she's talking on a phone?'

'Yes, yes, of course – using an invisible Bluetooth earpiece, you probably saw plenty of psychotic patients behaving just as flamboyantly during the last few years before you retired.'

Busner digested this remark for a while before responding, 'And plenty of people not on sections, simply wandering around in the city streets –' He would've continued, but the young woman was pointing vigorously at Mukti, who, with deft choreography, brought his face to within a foot of hers. 'I know – I *know*,' she expostulated, 'he's *such* a dish.' Then she tapped Mukti on the cheek and he withdrew a sheaf of papers from the breast pocket of his regulation psychiatric tweed jacket. While she slid the pad of her index finger over the same portion of nothingness again and again, as if drawing on water, he held first one sheet of paper then the next up in front of her. Busner said, 'What's going on?'

'Well,' Mukti explained, 'I've realised that when she taps like that on a physical object she's opening a sidebar – so I supply the text as she simulates scrolling down it. I've discovered that if I adjust my timing to hers she can actually take in what's written on the pages.'

'Which is?'

'Well, in this case – since it was me she tapped on – I'm

showing her the pages of my CV, but I usually have a file of newspaper clippings to hand. If I hold up a photograph she'll tap that and I'll follow it with the relevant article. Sometimes, when she's read this she'll sort of *highlight* a word or a phrase, and if I can catch what it is I'm able to cross-reference this with another article in the clippings file – the more I manage to do this, and the greater accuracy I achieve, the calmer she seems to become. She even . . .' and here Mukti's voice dropped to a reverent hush, awed as he was by his own therapeutic skill, '. . . stops talking on her invisible mobile.'

'Astonishing,' Busner remarked dryly.

'I tell you what I'm doing,' the woman patient spoke over them, loudly and coyly, 'I'm Googling my new shrink . . . No, no – there isn't much on him here . . . Pretty dull stuff, educated in Finchley . . . blah, blah, medical school . . . blah, blah, Shiva Mukti MD, MRCPsych . . . blah, blah – what? *What*!? No? Like, for real – ? I've got someone else calling, willya hold?' She doodled on a patch of the void local to her thigh while squealing, 'Mary? You'll never be-*lieve* who I'm talking to – yes, *right now*,' and simultaneously rapping Mukti smartly on the forehead, which, as he explained sotto voce to Busner, was the command for him to withdraw.

Regrouped in the corner of the treatment room the two mismatched soul doctors watched as the object of their enquiry juggled her two 'phone calls' for a few more minutes, before turning her attention to a spot in the mid-distance that she pincered apart into a vaporous cynosure. Fixating on this she nodded her head, tapped her foot on the scuzzy lino and began to mumble along in an abstracted way, 'Rejoice and love yourself today coz ba-by you were born this waay . . .'

'She's watching a video clip of a pop singer on

YouTube,' Mukti crowed, 'and I believe I know which one!'

'Oh,' Busner remained underwhelmed, 'and who's that then?'

'Lady Gaga!'

Later, seated in the basement canteen, Busner worked his way steadily through a plate piled high with rubbery eggs, greasy sausages, several scoops of mash, a raffia mat of bacon, a slurry of baked beans, a fungal growth of mushrooms, a disembowelling of stewed tomatoes – the entire mess suppurating sauce. Mukti looked on, appalled, and noticing his expression Busner confided: 'Y'know, you can take the man out of the institution – but after half a century odd, you can't deprive him altogether of the institutional food.'

Mukti lifted the dead mouse of his herbal teabag from his mug by its paper tail and regarded it balefully, 'Well,' he said. 'What do you make of my patient?'

'I suppose she has a name,' Busner said, 'I mean, she is a person y'know – not just a pathology.'

'Her name's Anna Richards. She's from a perfectly ordinary middle-class background, loving parents . . . siblings, friends – the whole bit. She was studying for an English degree at some provincial university when she had a flamboyant psychotic breakdown and started behaving like . . . like . . . well, like *this*. As I said, I've had a couple of others present in the last year with very similar symptoms, I've tentatively named it,' he gave a vaguely self-satisfied little moue, 'iPhrenia, so I tend to refer to her as –'

'iAnna, I s'pose.' With the nightmarish alacrity only witnessed in imperfectly constructed works of narrative fiction Busner had cleared his plate, and now he was mopping up the sloppy residuum with a triangle of bread as white as death. 'Humph,' he said through a mouthful, 'I admire your creative drive, Mukti, after all, given the metastasised malaise that passes for diagnostics in our field, coining a new name for an existing condition is as close as any of us is likely to get to immortality. But surely you cannot be unaware that every successive wave of technology has nightmarishly infected the psychotic? That in the preindustrial world they were possessed by devils and that once magnetism had been discovered their minds turned to the lodestone? When electricity appeared it immediately zapped their thoughts – and the coming of the telegraph dot–dot–dashed away on the inside of their skulls? This, um, *iPhrenia* is only the latest sad fancy to grip these distressed early-adopters, who have already been plagued by X-Rays and atomic bombs and Lord knows what else.'

During this little peroration the superannuated psychiatrist had risen, and he was already halfway across the canteen. 'Goodbye, Mukti,' he threw over his shoulder, 'please don't call me again, my mobile phone is sadly all too real –' but then something suddenly occurred to him, and he stopped, turned, then returned to the Melamine table with a flinty glint in his eye.

Up on the locked psychiatric ward of St Mungo's the distressed inmates rocked and rolled and eddied and howled in the zephyrs of their own fancy. It was a long, low-ceilinged chamber, poorly lit by a row of lancet windows. Surveying the gloomy scene Busner remarked testily: 'First we send these poor souls out to flap around the streets, and now we have nowhere for them but this *if* they're lucky enough to come home to roost.' Mukti grunted noncommittally – nearby a bored charge nurse stood, compulsively clicking a retractable Biro. On the unmade bed in front of the doctors sat iAnna, in a ghastly Terylene nightdress, performing her odd arabesques.

'It's only a hunch,' Busner said, turning his attention to her, 'but if, as you suggest, Mukti, for her the entire perceptual realm is mediated by these, ah, *motions*, surely it may be possible to . . .' With a surprising elegance Busner replicated on a larger scale a flurry of pointing, pinching and twisting that culminated with his outstretched fingers on the young woman's face. '. . . There!'

'Wow!' Mukti was taken aback. 'That's the first time I've seen her in repose since she arrived here – what did you do?'

'It's quite simple, I've reversed the screen-world so that Anna is now the computer, and we are its operators. She's dormant just now, but if I'm right, if I do this,' he tapped her on the forehead with a single finger, 'she will –'

Anna began chanting with the monotonous tone of a text-enabled electronic book: 'My name is An-na Rich-ards I am twenty-one I am curr-ent-ly in a men-tal hos-pi-tal I feel frigh-ten-ed and alone . . .' Speaking over her Busner said, 'Whereas if I do this,' with a second tap he silenced the patient, then lightly struck her shoulder. Again the monotonous voice, 'I was giv-en my Bee-Cee-Gee vacc-ci-na-tion when I was thir-teen I was scared of the nee-dle and a-no-ther girl teased and bull-ied me –' Busner tapped her into silence and straightening up said, 'Now, that is something genuinely novel, Mukti – a severely psychotic patient who can nonetheless furnish accurate and factual accounts of their own inner mental states. If you can manipulate iAnna effectively – rather than allowing her to play upon you – you may well end up with a research paper worthy of the British Journal of Ephemera.'

'W-won't you consider collaborating?' Mukti gasped.

'No . . . no, as I think I said to you on the phone, I'm retired now – I intend to cultivate my own neuroses the way other pensioners cultivate their allotments . . . but one other thing, Mukti.'

'What?'

For a few moments Busner stood staring down through the narrow, arched window into the mosh-pit of lunch-time central London, where a packed crowd of office prisoners had been let out for an hour's courtyard exercise. They bustled along talking to their invisible friends, or stood abstracted on the kerb the fingers of one hand fiddling away in the palm of the other, or, like iAnna footled fanatically with a filmy square-foot. Tearing himself away from the St Vitus' dance of modernity, Busner said, 'I have a suspicion that when you flip Anna around the other way again, if you actually provide her with an iPad of her own she'll be . . . well, if not exactly *cured* certainly capable of receiving care in the . . .' his moist amphibian lips dripped with distaste of the word '. . . community. No doubt your paper will do wonders in repairing the holes those palliative iPads will make in your savagely reduced budget.'

And with that, he was gone.

ALISON MACLEOD

The Heart of Denis Noble

A S DENIS NOBLE, Professor of Cardiovascular Physiology, succumbs to the opioids – a meandering river
of fentanyl from the IV drip – he is informed his heart is
on its way. In twenty, perhaps thirty minutes' time, the
Cessna air ambulance will land in the bright, crystalline
light of December, on the small landing-strip behind the
Radcliffe Hospital.

A bearded jaw appears over him. From this angle, the
mouth is oddly labial. Does he understand? Professor
Noble nods from the other side of the ventilation mask.
He would join in the team chat but the mask prevents it,
and in any case, he must lie still so the nurse can shave the
few hairs that remain on his chest.

No cool-box then. No heart on ice. This is what they
are telling him. Instead, the latest technology. He remembers the prototype he was once shown. His new heart will
arrive in its own state-of-the-art reliquary. It will be lifted,
beating, from a nutrient-rich bath of blood and oxygen.
So he can rest easy, someone adds. It's beating well at
40,000 feet, out of range of all turbulence. 'We need your
research, Professor,' another voice jokes from behind the
ECG. 'We're taking no chances!'

Which isn't to say that the whole thing isn't a terrible gamble.

The nurse has traded the shaver for a pair of nail-clippers. She sets to work on the nails of his right hand, his plucking hand. Is that necessary? he wants to ask. It will take him some time to grow them back, assuming of course he still has 'time'. As she slips the pulse-oximeter over his index finger, he wonders if Joshua will show any interest at all in the classical guitar he is destined to inherit, possibly any day now. According to his mother, Josh is into electronica and urban soul.

A second nurse bends and whispers in his ear like a lover. 'Now all you have to do is relax, Denis. We've got everything covered.' Her breath is warm. Her breast is near. He can imagine the gloss of her lips. He wishes she would stay by his ear for ever. 'We'll have you feeling like yourself again before you know it.'

He feels he might be sick.

Then his choice of pre-op music – the second movement of Schubert's *Piano Trio in E-Flat Major* – seems to flow, sweet and grave, from her mouth into his ear, and once more he can see past the red and golden treetops of Gordon Square to his attic room of half a century ago. A recording of the Schubert is rising through the floorboards, and the girl beside him in his narrow student bed is warm; her lips brush the lobe of his ear; her voice alone, the whispered current of it, is enough to arouse him. But when her fingers find him beneath the sheet, they surprise him with a catheter, and he has to shut his eyes against the tears, against the absurdity of age.

The heart of Denis Noble beat for the first time on the fifth of March, 1936 in the body of Ethel Noble as she stitched a breast pocket to a drape-cut suit in an upstairs room at Wilson & Jeffries, the tailoring house where she first met her husband George, a trainee cutter, across a flashing length of gold silk lining.

As she pierced the tweed with her basting needle, she remembered George's tender, awkward kiss to her collarbone that morning, and, as if in reply, Denis's heart, a mere tube at this point, beat its first of more than two billion utterances – da dum. Unknown to Ethel, she was twenty-one days pregnant. Her thread dangled briefly in mid-air.

Soon, the tube that was Denis Noble's heart, a delicate scrap of mesoderm, would push towards life. In the dark of Ethel, it would twist and grope, looping blindly back towards itself in the primitive knowledge that circulation, the vital whoosh of life, deplores a straight line. With a tube, true, we can see from end to end, we can blow clear through or whistle a tune – a tube is nothing if not straightforward – but a loop, a *loop*, is a circuit of energy understood only by itself.

In this unfolding, intra-uterine drama, Denis Noble – a dangling button on the thread of life – would begin to take shape, to hold fast. He would inherit George's high forehead and Ethel's bright almond-shaped, almost Oriental, eyes. His hands would be small but unusually dexterous. A birthmark would stamp itself on his left hip. But inasmuch as he was flesh, blood and bone, he was also, deep within Ethel, a living stream of sound and sensation, a delicate flux of stimuli, the influence of which eluded all known measure, then as now.

He was the cloth smoothed beneath Ethel's cool palm, and the pumping of her foot on the pedal of the Singer machine. He was the hiss of her iron over the sleeve press and the clink of brass pattern-weights in her apron pocket. He was the soft spring light through the open window, the warmth of it bathing her face, and the serotonin surging in her synapses at the sight of a magnolia tree in flower. He was the manifold sound-waves of passers-by: of motor cars hooting, of old men hawking and spitting, and delivery boys teetering down Savile Row under bolts of cloth bigger than they were. Indeed it is impossible to say where Denis stopped and the world began.

Only on a clear, cloudless night in November 1940 did the world seem to unstitch itself from the small boy he was and separate into something strange, something other. Denis opened his eyes to the darkness. His mother was scooping him from his bed and running down the stairs so fast, his head bumped up and down against her shoulder.

Downstairs, his father wasn't in his armchair with the newspaper on his lap, but on the sitting room floor cutting cloth by the light of a torch. Why was Father camping indoors? 'Let's sing a song,' his mother whispered, but she forgot to tell him which song to sing.

The kitchen was a dark place and no, it wasn't time for eggs and soldiers, not yet, she shooshed, and even as she spoke, she was depositing him beneath the table next to the fat yellow bundle that was his sister, and stretching out beside him, even though her feet in their court shoes stuck out the end. 'There, there,' she said as she pulled them both to her. Then they turned their ears towards a sky they couldn't see and listened to the planes that droned like wasps in the jar of the south London night.

When the bang came, the floor shuddered beneath them and plaster fell in lumps from the ceiling. His father rushed in from the sitting room, pins still gripped between his lips. Before his mother had finished thanking God, Denis felt his legs propel him, without permission, not even his own, to the window to look. Beneath a corner of the black-out curtain, at the bottom of the garden, flames were leaping. 'Fire!' he shouted, but his father shouted louder, nearly swallowing his pins – 'GET AWAY from the window!' – and plucked him into the air.

They owed their lives, his mother would later tell Mrs West next door, to a cabinet minister's suit. Their Anderson shelter, where they would have been huddled were it not for the demands of bespoke design, had taken a direct hit.

That night, George and a dicky stirrup-pump waged a losing battle against the flames until neighbours joined in with rugs, hoses and buckets of sand. Denis stood behind his mother's hip at the open door. His baby sister howled from her Moses basket. Smoke gusted as he watched his new red wagon melt in the heat. Ethel smiled down at him, squeezing his hand, and it seemed very odd because his mother shook as much as she smiled and she smiled as much as she shook. It should have been very difficult, like rubbing your tummy and patting your head at the same time, and as Denis beheld his mother – her eyes wet with tears, her hair unpinned, her arms goose-pimpled – he felt something radiate through his chest. The feeling was delicious. It warmed him through. He felt light on his toes. If his mother hadn't been wearing her heavy navy blue court shoes, the two of them, he thought, might have floated off the doorstep and into the night.

At the same time, the feeling was an ache, a hole, a sore inside him. It made him feel heavy. His heart was like something he'd swallowed that had gone down the wrong way. It made it hard to breathe. Denis Noble, age four, didn't understand. As the tremor in his mother's arm travelled into his hand, up his arm, through his armpit and into his chest, he felt for the first time the mysterious life of the heart.

He had of course been briefed in the weeks prior to surgery. His consultant, Mr Bonham, had sat at his desk – chins doubling with the gravity of the situation – reviewing Denis's notes. The tests had been inconclusive but the 'rather urgent' need for transplantation remained clear.

Naturally he would, Mr Bonham said, be familiar with the procedure. An incision in the ribcage. The removal of the pericardium – 'a slippery business, but routine'. Denis's heart would be emptied, and the aorta clamped prior to excision. Textbook. The chest cavity would be cleared, though the biatrial cuff would be left in place. Then the new heart would be 'unveiled – voilà!', and the aorta engrafted, followed by the pulmonary artery.

Most grafts, Mr Bonham assured him, recovered normal ventricular function without intervention. There were risks, of course: bleeding, RV failure, bradyarrhythmias, conduction abnormalities, sudden death . . .

Mr Bonham surveyed his patient through his half-moon specs. 'Atheist, I presume?'

'I'm afraid not.' Denis regarded his surgeon with polite patience. Mr Bonham was widely reputed to be one of the last eccentrics still standing in the NHS.

'A believer then. Splendid. More expedient at times like this. And fear not. The Royal Society won't hear it from me!'

'Which is perhaps just as well,' said Denis, 'as I'm afraid I make as poor a "believer" as I do an atheist.'

Mr Bonham removed his glasses. 'Might be time to sort the muddle out.' He huffed on his specs, gave them a wipe with a crumpled handkerchief, and returned them to the end of his nose. 'I have a private hunch, you see, that agnostics don't fare quite as well in major surgery.

No data for *The Lancet* as yet but' – he ventured a wink – 'even so. See if you can't muster a little . . . certainty.'

A smile crept across Denis's face. 'The Buddhists advise against too much metaphysical certainty.'

'You're a Buddhist?' A Buddhist at Oxford? At Balliol?'

Denis's smile strained. 'I try to keep my options open.'

'I see.' Mr Bonham didn't. There was an embarrassment of categories. A blush spread up his neck, and as Denis watched his surgeon shuffle his notes, he felt his chances waver.

The *allegro* now. The third movement of the *Piano Trio* – *faster, faster* – but the Schubert is receding, and as Denis surfaces from sleep, he realises he's being whisked down the wide, blanched corridors of the Heart Unit. His trolley is a precision vehicle. It glides. It shunts around corners. There's no time to waste – the heart must be fresh – and he wonders if he has missed his stop. Kentish Town. Archway. Highgate. East Finchley. The names of the stations flicker past like clues in a dream to a year he cannot quite summon. Tunnel after tunnel. He mustn't nod off again, mustn't miss the stop, but the carriage is swaying and rocking, it's only quarter past five in the morning, and it's hard to resist the ramshackle lullaby of the Northern Line.

West Finchley. Woodside Park.

1960.

That's the one.

It's 1960, but no one, it seems, has told the good people of Totteridge. Each time he steps onto the platform at the quaint, well swept station, he feels as if he has been catapulted back in time.

The slaughterhouse is a fifteen-minute walk along a

B-road, and Denis is typically the first customer of the day. He feels under-dressed next to the workers in their whites, their hard hats, their metal aprons and steel-toed Wellies. They stare, collectively, at his loafers.

Slaughter-men aren't talkers by nature, but nevertheless, over the months, Denis has come to know each by name. Front of house, there's Alf the Shackler, Frank the Knocker, Jimmy the Sticker, Marty the Plucker, and Mike the Splitter. Frank tells him how, years ago, a sledge-hammer saw him through the day's routine, but now it's a pneumatic gun and a bolt straight to the brain; a few hundred shots a day, which means he has to wear goggles, 'cos of all the grey matter flying'. He's worried he's developing 'trigger-finger', and he removes his plastic glove so Denis can see for himself 'the finger what won't uncurl'.

Alf is brawny but soft-spoken with kind, almost womanly eyes. Every morning on the quiet, he tosses Denis a pair of Wellies to spare his shoes. No one mentions the stink of the place, a sharp kick to the lungs of old blood, manure and offal. The breeze-block walls exhale it and the floor reeks of it, even though the place is mopped down like a temple every night.

Jimmy is too handsome for a slaughterhouse, all dirty blond curls and American teeth, but he doesn't know it because he's a farmboy who's never been further than East Finchley. Marty, on the other hand, was at Dunkirk. He has a neck like a battering ram and a lump of shrapnel in his head. Every day, at the close of business, he brings his knife home with him on the passenger seat of his Morris Mini-Minor. He explains to Denis that he spends a solid hour each night sharpening and sanding the blade to make sure it's smooth with no pits. 'An' 'e wonders,' bellows Mike, 'why 'e can't get a bird!'

Denis pays £4 for two hearts a day, a sum that left

him stammering with polite confusion on his first visit. At Wilson and Jeffries, his father earns £20 per week.

Admittedly, they bend the rules for him. Frank 'knocks' the first sheep as usual. Alf shackles and hoists. But Jimmy, who grasps his sticking knife – Jimmy, the youngest, who's always keen, literally, to 'get stuck in' – doesn't get to slit the throat and drain the animal. When Denis visits, there's a different protocol. Jimmy steps aside, and Marty cuts straight into the chest and scoops out 'the pluck'. The blood gushes. The heart and lungs steam in Marty's hands. The others tssk-tssk like old women at the sight of the spoiled hide, but Marty is butchery in motion. He casts the lungs down a chute, passes the warm heart to Denis, rolls the stabbed sheep down the line to Mike the Splitter, shouts 'Chop, chop, ha ha' at Mike, and waits like a veteran for Alf to roll the second sheep his way.

Often Denis doesn't wait to get back to the lab. He pulls a large pair of scissors from his hold-all, grips the heart at arm's length, cuts open the meaty ventricles, checks to ensure the Purkinje fibres are still intact, then pours a steady stream of Tyrode solution over and into the heart. When the blood is washed clear, he plops the heart into his Thermos and waits for the next heart as the gutter in the floor fills with blood. The Tyrode solution, which mimics the sugar and salts of blood, is a simple but strange elixir. Denis still can't help but take a schoolboy sort of pleasure in its magic. There in his Thermos, at the core of today's open heart, the Purkinje fibres have started to beat again in their Tyrode bath. Very occasionally, a whole ventricle comes to life as he washes it down. On those occasions, he lets Jimmy hold the disembodied heart as if it is a wounded bird fluttering between his palms.

Then the Northern Line flickers past in reverse until Euston Station re-appears, where Denis hops out and jogs

– Thermos and scissors clanging in the hold-all – down Gower Street, past the main quad, through the Anatomy entrance, up the grand, century-old staircase to the second floor, and into the empty lab before the clock on the wall strikes seven.

In the hush of the Radcliffe's principal operating theatre, beside the anaesthetised, intubated body of Denis Noble, Mr Bonham assesses the donor heart for a final time.

The epicardial surface is smooth and glistening. The quantity of fat is negligible. The aorta above the valve reveals a smooth intima with no atherosclerosis. The heart is still young, after all; sadly, just seventeen years old, though – in keeping with protocol – he has revealed nothing of the donor identity to the patient, and Professor Noble knows better than to ask. The lumen of the coronary artery is large, without any visible narrowing. The muscular arterial wall is of sound proportion.

Pre-operative monitoring has confirmed strong wall motion, excellent valve function, good conduction and regular heart rhythm.

It's a ticklish business at the best of times, he reminds his team, but yes, he is ready to proceed.

In the lab of the Anatomy Building, Denis pins out the heart like a valentine in a Petri dish. The buried trove, the day's booty, is nestled at the core; next to the red flesh of the ventricle, the Purkinje network is a skein of delicate yellow fibres. They gleam like the bundles of pearl cotton his mother used to keep in her embroidery basket.

Locating them is one thing. Getting them is another. It is tricky work to lift them free; trickier still to cut away sections without destroying them. He needs a good eye, a small pair of surgical scissors, and the steady cutting hand he inherited, he likes to think, from his father. If impatience gets the better of him, if he sneezes, if his scissors slip, it will be a waste of a fresh and costly heart. Beyond the lab door, an undergrad class thunders down the staircase. Outside, through the thin Victorian glass panes, Roy Orbison croons 'Only the Lonely' on a transistor radio.

Denis drops his scissors and reaches for a pair of forceps. He works like a watchmaker, lifting another snipped segment free. A second Petri dish awaits. A fresh bath of Tyrode solution, an oxygenated variety this time, will boost their recovery. If all goes well, he can usually harvest a dozen segments from each heart. But the ends will need to close before the real work can begin. Sometimes they need an hour, sometimes longer.

Coffee. He needs a coffee. He boils water on the Bunsen burner someone pinched from the chemistry lab. The instant coffee is on the shelf with the belljars. He pours, using his sleeve as a mitt, and, in the absence of a spoon, uses the pencil that's always tucked behind his ear.

At the vast chapel-arch of a window, he can just see the treetops of Gordon Square, burnished with autumn, and far below, the gardeners raking leaves and lifting bulbs. Beyond it, from this height, he can see as far as Tavistock Square, though the old copper beech stands between him and a view of his own attic window at the top of Connaught Hall.

He tries not to think about Ella, whom he hopes to find, several hours from now, on the other side of that window, in his room – i.e., his bed – where they have agreed to meet to 'compare the findings' of their respective days. Ella, a literature student, has been coolly bluffing her way into the Press Box at the Old Bailey for the last week or so. For his part, he'd never heard of the infamous novel until the headlines got hold of it, but Ella is gripped and garrulous, and even the sound of her voice in his ear fills him with a desire worthy of the finest dirty book.

He paces, mug in hand. He can't bring himself to leave his fibres unattended while they heal.

He watches the clock.

He checks the fibres. Too soon.

He deposits his mug on the window sill and busies himself with his prep. He fills the first glass micro-pipette with potassium chloride, inserts the silver thread-wire and connects it to the valve on his home-made amp. The glass pipette in his hand always brings to mind the old wooden dibber, smooth with use, that his father used during spring planting. Denis can see him still, in his weekend pull-over and tie, on his knees in the garden, as he dibbed and dug for a victory that was in no hurry to come. Only his root vegetables ever rewarded his efforts.

Soon, Antony and Günter, his undergrad assistants, will shuffle in for duty. He'll post Antony, with the camera and a stockpile of film, at the oscilloscope's screen. Günter will take to the dark room next to the lab, and emerge pale and blinking at the end of the day.

Outside, the transistor radio and its owner take their leave. He drains his coffee, glances at the clock, and checks his nails for sheep's blood. How much longer? He allows himself to wander as far as the stairwell and back again. He doodles on the blackboard – a sickle moon, a tree, a stick man clinging to a branch – and erases all three.

At last, at last. He prepares a slide, sets up the Zeiss, switches on its light and swivels the lens into place. At this magnification, the fibre cells are pulsing minnows of life. His 'dibbers' are ready; Günter passes him the first and checks its connection to the amp. Denis squints over the Zeiss and inserts the micro-pipette into a cell membrane. The view is good. He can even spot the two boss-eyed nuclei. If the second pipette penetrates the cell success-fully, he'll make contact with the innermost life of the cell.

His wrist is steady, which means every impulse, every rapid-fire excitation, should travel up the pipette through the thread-wire and into the valve of the amplifier. The oscilloscope will 'listen' to the amp. Fleeting waves of voltage will rise and fall across its screen, and Antony will snap away on the Nikon, capturing every fluctua-tion, every trace. Günter, for his part, has already removed himself like a penitent to the dark room. There, if all goes well, he'll capture the divine spark of life on Kodak paper, over and over again.

Later still, they'll convert the electrical ephemera of the day into scrolling graphs; they'll chart the unfolding peaks and troughs; they'll watch on paper the ineffable currents that compel the heart to life.

Cell after cell. Impulse upon impulse. An ebb and flow of voltage. The unfolding story of a single heartbeat in thousandths of a second.

'Tell me,' says Ella, 'about your excitable cells. I like those.' Their heads share the one pillow. Schubert's piano trio is rising through the floorboards of the student hall. A cellist he has yet to meet lives below.

'I'll give you excitable.' He pinches her bottom. She bites the end of his nose. Through the crack of open window, they can smell trampled leaves, wet pave-ment and frost-bitten earth. In the night above the attic window, the stars throb.

She sighs luxuriously and shifts, so that Denis has to grip the mattress of the narrow single bed to steady himself. 'Excuse me, Miss, but I'm about to go over the edge.'

'Of the bed or your mental health? Have you found those canals yet?'

'Channels.'

'Precisely. Plutonium channels. See? I listen. You might not think I do, but I do.'

'Potassium. Potassium channels.'

'That's what I said.'

'I'm afraid you didn't. Which means . . .'

'Which means . . .?'

He rumples his brow in a display of forethought. 'Which means – and I say this with regret – I might just have to spank you.' He marvels at his own audacity. He is someone new with her and, at the same time, he has never felt more himself.

'Cheek!' she declares, and covers her own with the eiderdown. 'But I'm listening now. Tell me again. What do you do with these potassium channels?'

'I map their electrical activity. I demonstrate the movement of ions – electrically charged particles – through the cell membranes.' From the mattress edge, he gets a purchase by grabbing hold of her hip.

'Why aren't you more pleased?'

'Tell me about the trial today.'

'I thought you said those channels of yours were *the* challenge. The new discovery. The biologist's New World.'

'I'm pleased. Yes. Thanks. It's going well.' He throws back the eiderdown, springs to his feet and rifles through her shoulder bag for her notebook. 'Is it in here?'

'Is what?'

'Your notebook.'

'A man's testicles are never at their best as he bends,' she observes.

'So did The Wigs put on a good show today?'

She folds her arms across the eiderdown. 'I'm not

talking dirty until you tell me about your potassium what-nots.'

'Channels.' From across the room, his back addresses her. 'They're simply passages or pores in the cell membrane that allow a mass of charged ions to be shunted into the cell – or out of it again if there's an excess.'

She sighs. 'If it's all so matter of fact, why are you bothering?'

He returns to her side, kisses the top of her head and negotiates his way back into the bed. 'My supervisor put me on the case, and, like I say, all's well. I'm getting the results, rather more quickly than I expected, so I'm pleased. Relieved even. Because in truth, I would have looked a little silly if I hadn't found them. They're already known to exist in muscle cells, and the heart is only another muscle after all.'

'Only another muscle?'

'Yes.' He flips through her notebook.

'But this is something that has you running through Bloomsbury in the middle of the night and leaving me for a date with a computer.'

He kisses her shoulder. 'The computer isn't nearly so amiable.'

'Denis Noble, are you doing interesting work or aren't you?'

'I have a dissertation to produce.'

'Please. Never be, you know . . . take it or leave it. Never be bored. Men who are bored bore me.'

'Then I shall stifle every yawn.'

'You'll have to do better than that. Tell me what you aim to discover next.' She divests him of his half of the eiderdown, and he grins, in spite of the cold.

'Whatever it is, you'll be the first to know.'

'Perhaps it isn't an "it",' she muses. 'Have you thought of that?'

'How can "it" not be an "it"?'

'I'm not sure,' she says, and she wraps herself up like the Queen of Sheba. The eiderdown crackles with static, and her fine, shiny hair flies away in the light of the desk-lamp. 'But a book, for example, is not an "it".'

'Of course it's an "it". It's an object, a thing. Ask any girl in her deportment class, as she walks about with one on her head.'

'Then I'll re-phrase, shall I? A story is not an "it". If it's any good, it's more alive than an "it". Every part of a great story "contains" every other part. Every small part anticipates the whole. Nothing can be passive or static. Nothing is just a part. Not really. Because the whole, if it's powerful enough that is, cannot be divided. That's what a great creation is. It has its own marvellous unity.' She pauses to examine the birthmark on his hip, a new discovery. 'Of course, I'm fully aware I sound like a) a girl and b) a dreamy arts student, but I suspect the heart *is* a great creation and that the same rule applies.'

'And which *rule* might that be?' He loves listening to her, even if he has no choice but to mock her, gently.

'The same principle then.'

He raises an eyebrow.

She adjusts her generous breasts. 'The principle of Eros. Eros is an attractive force. It binds the world; it makes connections. At best, it gives way to a sense of whole-ness, a sense of the sacred even; at worst, it leads to fuzzy vision. Logos, your contender, particularises. It makes the elements of the world distinct. At best, it is illuminat-ing; at worst, it is reductive. It cheapens. Both are vital. The balance is the thing. You need Eros, Denis. You're missing Eros.'

He passes her her notebook and taps it. 'On that point, we agree entirely. I wait with the utmost patience.'

She studies him with suspicion, then opens the spiral-bound stenographer's notebook. In the days before the trial, she taught herself shorthand in record time simply to capture, like any other putative member of the press, the banned passages of prose. She was determined to help carry their erotic charge into the world. 'T.S. Eliot was supposed to give evidence for the defence today, but apparently he sat in his taxi and couldn't bring himself to "do the deed".'

'Old men – impotent. Young men' – he smiles shyly and nods to his exposed self – 'ready.' He opens her notebook to a random page of shorthand. The ink is purple.

'My little joke,' she says. 'A sense of humour is *de rigueur* in the Press Box.' She nestles into the pillow and relinquishes his half of the eiderdown. He pats down her fly-away hair. 'From Chapter Ten,' she begins. ' "Then with a quiver of exquisite pleasure he touched the warm soft body, and touched her navel for a moment in a kiss. And he had to come into her at once, to enter the peace on earth of her soft quiescent body. It was the moment of pure peace for him, the entry into the body of a woman." '

'That gamekeeper chap doesn't hang about,' he says, his smile twitching.

'Quiet,' she chides. 'He is actually a very noble sort. Not sordid like you.'

'My birth certificate would assure you that I'm a Noble sort.'

'Ha ha.'

Denis lays his head against her breast and listens to the beat of her heart as she reads. Her voice enters him like a current and radiates through him until he feels himself almost hum with it, as if he is the body of a violin or cello that exists only to amplify her voice. He suspects he is not in love with her – and that is really just as well – but it occurs to him that he has never known such sweetness, such delight. He tries to stay in the moment, to loiter in the beats between the words she reads, between the breaths she takes. He runs his hand over the bell of her hip and tries not to think that in just four hours he will set off into the darkened streets of Bloomsbury, descend a set of basement steps and begin his night shift in the company of the only computer at the University of London that is powerful enough to crunch his milliseconds of data into readable equations.

As a lowly biologist, an ostensible lightweight among the physicists and computer guys, he has been allocated the least enviable slot on the computer, from two till four am. By five, he'll be on the Northern Line again, heading for the slaughterhouse.

Ella half wakes as he leaves.

'Go back to sleep,' he whispers. He grabs his jacket and the hold-all.

She sits up in bed, blinking in the light of the lamp which he has turned to the wall. 'Are you going now?'

'Yes.' He smiles, glancing at her, finds his wallet and checks he has enough for the hearts of the day.

'Goodbye, Denis,' she says softly.

'Sweet dreams,' he says.

But she doesn't stretch and settle back under the eider-down. She remains upright and naked even though the room is so cold, their breath has turned to frost on the inside of the window. He wonders if there isn't something odd in her expression. He hovers for a moment before deciding it is either a shadow from the lamp or the residue of a dream. Whatever the case, he can't be late for his shift. If he is, the porter in the unit won't be there to let him in – which means he has no more time to think on it.

He switches off the lamp.

In his later years, Denis Noble has allowed himself to wonder, privately, about the physiology of love. He has loved – with gratitude and frustration – parents, siblings, a spouse and two children. What, he asks himself, is love if not a force within? And what is a force within if not something *lived through* the body? Nevertheless, as Emeritus Professor of Cardiovascular Physiology, he has to admit he knows little more about love than he did on the night he fell in love with his mother; the night their shelter was bombed; the night he felt with utter certainty the strange and secret life of the heart within his chest.

Before 1960 drew to a close, he would – like hundreds of thousands of other liberated readers – buy the banned book and try to understand it as Ella had understood it. Later still in life, he would dedicate himself to the music and poetry of the Occitan troubadours. ('*I only know the grief that comes to me, to my love-ridden heart, out of over-loving . . .*') He would read and re-read the ancient sacred-sexual texts of the Far East. He would learn, almost by heart, St. Theresa's account of her vision of the seraph: '*I saw in his hands a long spear of gold, and at the iron's point there seemed to be a little fire. He appeared to me to be thrusting it at times into my heart, and to pierce my very entrails; when he drew it out, he seemed to draw them out also, and to leave me all on fire with a great love of God. The pain was so great that it made me moan; and yet so surpassing was the sweetness of this excessive pain that I could not wish to be rid of it.*'

But *what*, he wanted to ask St. Theresa, could the heart, that feat of flesh, blood and voltage, have to do with love? *Where*, he'd like to know, is love? *How* is love?

❧

On the train to Totteridge, he can still smell the citrus of Ella's perfume on his hands, in spite of all the punched paper-tape offerings he's been feeding to the computer through the night. He only left its subterranean den an hour ago. These days, the slots of his schedule are his daily commandments.

He is allowed 'to live' and to sleep from seven each evening to half past one the next morning, when his alarm wakes him for his shift in the computer unit. He closes the door on the darkness of Connaught Hall and sprints across Bloomsbury. After his shift, he travels from the Comp. Science basement to the Northern Line, from the Northern Line to the slaughterhouse, from the slaughterhouse to Euston, and from Euston to the lab for his twelve-hour day. 'Seven to seven,' he declares to his supervisor. He arrives home to Connaught Hall for supper at seven-thirty, Ella at eight, sleep at ten and three hours' oblivion until the alarm rings and the cycle starts all over again.

He revels briefly in the thought of a pretty girl still asleep in his bed, a luxury he'd never dared hope to win as a science student. Through the smeared carriage windows, the darkness is thinning into a murky dawn. The Thermos jiggles in the hold-all at his feet, the carriage door rattles and clangs, and his head falls back.

Up ahead, Ella is standing naked and grand on a bright woodland path in Tavistock Square. She doesn't seem to care that she can be seen by all the morning commuters and the students rushing past on their way to classes. She slips through the gate at the western end of the square and turns, closing it quickly. As he reaches it, he realises it is a kissing-gate. She stands on the other side but refuses him her lips. 'Gates open,' she says tenderly, 'and they close.'

He tries to go through but she shakes her head. When he pulls on the gate, he gets an electric shock. 'Why are you surprised?' she says. Then she's disappearing through another gate into Gordon Square, and her hair is flying-away in the morning light, as if she herself is electric. He pulls again on the gate, but it's rigid.

The dream returns to him only later as Marty is scooping the pluck from the first sheep on the line.

He feels again the force of that electric shock.

The gate was conductive . . .

It opened . . . It closed.

It *closed*.

He receives from Marty the first heart of the day. It's hot between his palms but he doesn't reach for his scissors. He doesn't open the Thermos. He hardly moves. Deep within him, it's as if his own heart has been jump-started to life.

In the operating theatre, Mr Bonham and his team have been at work for three-and-a-half hours, when at last he gives the word. Professor Noble can be disconnected from the bypass machine. His pulse is strong. The new heart, declares Mr Bonham, 'is going great guns'.

His dream of Ella at the gate means he can't finish at the slaughterhouse quickly enough. On the train back into town, he swears under his breath at the eternity of every stop. In the lab, he wonders if the ends of the Purkinje fibres will ever close and heal. He has twelve hours of lab time. Seven to seven. Will it be enough?

Twelve hours pass like two. The fibres are tricky today. He botched more than a few in the dissection, and the insertion of the micro-pipette has been hit and miss. Antony and Günter exchange looks. They discover he has amassed untold quantities of film, and he tells Antony he wants a faster shutter speed. When they request a lunch break, he simply stares into the middle distance. When Günter complains that his hands are starting to burn from the fixatives, Denis looks up from his micro-pipette, as if at a tourist who requires something of him in another language.

Finally, when the great window is a chapel arch of darkness and rain, he closes and locks the lab door behind him. There is nothing in his appearance to suggest anything other than a long day's work. No one he passes on the grand staircase of the Anatomy Building pauses to look. No one glances back, pricked by an intuition or an after-thought. He has remembered his hold-all and the Thermos for tomorrow's hearts. He has forgotten his jacket, but the sight of a poorly dressed student is nothing to make anyone look twice.

Yet as he steps into the downpour of the night, every light is blazing in his head. His brain is Piccadilly Circus, and in the dazzle, he hardly sees where he's going but he's running, across Gordon Square and on towards Tavistock . . . He wants to shout the news to the winos who shelter from the rain under dripping trees. He wants to holler it to every lit window, to every student in his or her numinous haze of thought. He wants to dash up the stairs of Connaught Hall, knock on the door of the mystery cellist, and blurt out the words. Tomorrow at the slaughterhouse, he tells himself, he might even have to hug Marty and Alf. 'They *close*!'

He saw it with his own eyes: potassium channels that *closed*.

They did just the opposite of what everyone expected.

He assumed some sort of experimental error. He went back through Günter's contact sheets. He checked the amp and the connections. He wondered if he wasn't merely observing his own wishful thinking. He started again. He shook things up. He subjected the cells to change – changes of voltage, of ions, of temperature. Antony asked, morosely, for permission to leave early. He had an exam – Gross Anatomy – the next day. Didn't Antony understand? 'They're not simply open,' he announced over a new ten-pound cylinder of graph paper. 'They *opened*.'

Antony's face was blank as an egg.

Günter suggested they call it a day.

But the channels opened. They were active. They opened *and*, more remarkably still, they *closed*.

Ella was right. He'll tell her she was. He'll be the first to admit it. The channels aren't merely passive conduits. They're not just machinery or component parts. They're alive and responsive.

Too many ions inside the cell – too much stress, exercise, anger, love, lust or despair – and they close. They stop all incoming electrical traffic. They preserve calm in the midst of too much life. They allow the ion gradient to stabilise.

He can hardly believe it himself. The heart 'listens' to itself. Causation isn't just upward; it's unequivocally downward too. It's a beautiful loop of feedback. The parts of the heart listen to each other as surely as musicians in an ensemble listen to each other. That's what he's longing to tell Ella. *That's* what he's discovered. Forget the ensemble. The heart is an *orchestra*. It's the BBC Proms. It's the Boston Pops. Even if he only understands its rhythm section today, he knows this now. The heart is infinitely more than the sum of its parts.

And he can prove it mathematically. The super computer will vouch for him, he feels sure of it. He'll design the equations. He'll come up with a computer model that will make even the physicists and computer scientists stand and gawp.

Which is when it occurs to him: what if the heart doesn't stop at the heart? What if the connections don't end?

Even he doesn't quite know what he means by this.

He will ask Ella. He will tell her of their meeting at the kissing-gate. He will ask for the kiss her dream-self refused him this morning. He'll enjoy the sweet confusion on her face.

Ella at eight.

Ella always at eight.

He waits by the window until the lights go out over Tavistock Square and the trees melt into darkness.

He waits for three days. He retreats under the eiderdown. He is absent from the slaughterhouse, the lab and the basement.

A fortnight passes. A month. The new year.

When the second movement of the *Piano Trio* rises through the floorboards, he feels nothing. It has taken him months, but finally, he feels nothing.

As he comes round, the insult of the tube down his throat assures him he hasn't died.

The first thing he sees is his grandson by the foot of his bed tapping away on his new mobile phone. 'Hi Granddad,' Josh says, as if Denis has only been napping. He bounces to the side of the ICU bed, unfazed by the bleeping monitors and the tubes. 'Put your index finger here, Denis. I'll help you . . . No, like right *over* the camera lens. That's it. This phone has an Instant Heart Rate App. We'll see if you're working yet.'

'Cool,' Denis starts to say, but the irony is lost to the tube in his throat.

Josh's brow furrows. He studies his phone screen like a doctor on a medical soap. 'Sixty-two beats per minute at rest. Congratulations, Granddad. You're like . . . alive.' Josh squeezes his hand and grins.

Denis has never been so glad to see him.

On the other side of the bed, his wife touches his shoulder. Her face is tired. The fluorescence of the lights age her. She has lipstick on her front tooth and tears in her eyes as she bends to whisper, hoarsely, in his ear. 'You came back to me.'

The old words.

After a week, he'd given up hope. He realised he didn't even know where she lived, which student residence, which flat, which telephone exchange. He'd never thought to ask. Once he even tried waiting for her outside the Old Bailey, but the trial was over, someone told him. Days before. Didn't he read the papers?

When she opened his door in January of '61, she stood on the threshold, like an apparition who might at any moment disappear again. She simply waited, her shiny hair still flying away from her in the light of the bare bulb on the landing. He was standing at the window through which he'd given up looking. On the other side, the copper beech was bare with winter. In the room below, the Schubert recording was stuck on a scratch.

Her words, when they finally came, were hushed and angry. They rose and fell in a rhythm he'd almost forgotten. 'Why don't you *know* that you're in love with me? What's wrong with you, Denis Noble?'

Cooking smells – boiled vegetables and mince – wafted into his room from the communal kitchen on the floor below. It seemed impossible that she should be here. Ella. Not Ella at eight. *Ella.*

Downstairs, the cellist moved the needle on the record.

'You came back to me,' he said.

His eyes filled.

As his recuperation begins, he will realise, with not a little impatience, that he knows nothing at all about the whereabouts of love. He knows only where it isn't. It is not in the heart, or if it is, it is not only in the heart. The organ that first beat in the depths of Ethel in the upstairs room of Wilson & Jeffries is now consigned to the scrap-heap of cardiovascular history. Yet in this moment, with a heart that is not strictly his, he loves Ella as powerfully as he did the night she re-appeared in his room on Tavistock Square.

But if love is not confined to the heart, nor would it seem is memory confined to the brain. The notion tantalises him. Those aspects or qualities which make the human condition human – love, consciousness, memory, affinity – are, Denis feels more sure than ever, *distributed* throughout the body. The single part, as Ella once claimed so long ago, must contain the whole.

He hopes his new heart will let him live long enough to see the proof. He'll have to chivvy the good folk at the Physiome Project along.

He wishes he had a pencil.

In the meantime, as Denis adjusts to his new heart hour by hour, day by day, he will demonstrate, in Josh's steadfast company, an imperfect but unprecedented knowledge of the lyrics of Jay-Z and OutKast. He will announce to Ella that he is keen to buy a BMX bike. He won't be sure himself whether he is joking or not. He will develop an embarrassing appetite for doner kebabs, and he will not be deterred by the argument, put to him by Ella, his daughter and Josh, that he has never eaten a doner kebab in his entire life.

He will surprise even himself when he hears himself tell
Mr Bonham, during his evening rounds, that he favours
Alton Towers over the Dordogne this year.

We Wave and Call

A ND SOMETIMES IT happens like this: a young man
lying face down in the ocean, his limbs hanging
loosely beneath him, a motorboat droning slowly across
the bay, his body moving in long, slow ripples with each
passing shallow wave, the water moving softly across his
skin, muffled shouts carrying out across the water, and
the electric crackle of waves sliding up against the rocks
and birds in the trees and the body of a young man lying
in the ocean, face down and breathlessly still.

You open your eyes, blinking against the light which
pulses through the water. You look down at the sea floor,
hearing only the hollow suck and sigh of your own breath
through the snorkel, seeing the broken shells, the rusting
beer cans, the polished pieces of broken glass. Black-
spiked sea urchins clinging to the rocks. Tiny black fish
moving through the sea-grass. A carrier bag tumbling in
tight circles at the foot of the shoreline rocks. You hold
out your hands, seeing how pale they look in the water,
the skin of your fingers beginning to pucker a little. The
sea feels as warm as bath water, and you're almost drifting
off to sleep when you hear the sudden smack and plunge
of something hitting the water nearby.

You turn your head, and see a young boy sinking through the water, his knees to his chest and his eyes squeezed shut. Above, way up in the air, another three boys are falling from a high rocky outcrop, their shorts ballooning out around their hips, their hair rising, their mouths held open in anticipatory cries. One of them flaps his hands, trying to slow his fall. The other two reach out and touch the tips of their fingers together. All three of them look down at the water with something like fear and joy.

Your friends are watching as well, sprawled across a wide concrete ledge jutting out over the sea. Claire turns and looks for you, waving, brushing the knots from her wet tangled hair. Her pale skin is shiny with sun cream and seawater.

'We're making a move now,' she calls; 'you coming?'

The others are already standing up, brushing bits of dirt from their skin and shaking out their towels. You lift the mask from your face and take the snorkel from your mouth and tell her you're staying in a bit longer. You'll catch them up in a minute, you say.

They pick up the sun cream and water bottles, the paperback books, the leaflets from the tourist information office in town. The girls lift up their damp hair, squeezing out the water and letting it run down their backs. Andy buttons his shirt and steps into his unlaced trainers.

'We're not waiting for you,' Claire says. You wave her off and say that's fine. You'll be out in a minute or two.

The night before, sitting at a table outside one of the cafés in the old town, the girls had got up to go to the toilet together, leaving their tall glasses of beer on the table and tugging at their skirts. Andy had caught your eye, and lifted his drink in salute, and you'd both smiled broadly at your good fortune. Nothing had needed to be said. You'd left behind long months of exams and anxieties in the flat grey east of England and landed suddenly in this new world of cheap beer and sunshine, of clear blue seas and girls who wore bikinis and short skirts and slept in the room next door. It felt like something you'd both been waiting years for; something you've long been promised. It felt like adulthood. The girls have already made it clear, by their pointing out of waiters and boys on scooters, that they're more interested in the locals than in the two of you. But there's still a chance. A feeling that something could happen; that anything could happen. It seems worth thinking about, at least.

You put the mask over your eyes and lie back in the water for a while, looking up at the steep sides of the bay, kicking your legs to send yourself drifting away from the rocks. You're not sure you ever want to get out. At home, the beach is a few minutes away, and you've grown up running in and out of the sea. But you've never really swum; there, you run in, shouting against the shock of the cold, and run out again as soon as you can. Here, you could sleep in the clear warm water. You watch the others making their way up the path between the pine trees and oleander bushes. A bus drives along the road at the top of the hillside, stops near the gap in the railings, and moves off. A young couple on a scooter overtake it, the boy riding without a shirt or a helmet, the girl wearing a knee-length wraparound skirt and a bikini top, her hair flowing out behind her. Birds hang still in the warm currents of air drifting up the side of the hill. The grasshoppers sound out their steady scraping shriek. The air is thick with the scent of crushed pine needles and scorched rosemary, heavy with heat.

Along the bay, at the bottom of a steep flight of steps

cut straight from the rock, there's another small bathing jetty. A girl in a black swimming costume sits on the edge, her feet in the water, a white towel hanging over her head, reading a book.

Further along, where the bay curves round to form a long headland jutting out into the sea, there's an ugly concrete hotel with its name spelt out in white sky-line letters. Half the letters are missing, and when you look again you see that the whole building is a ruin: the windows shot to pieces, gaping holes blown in the walls, coils of barbed wire rolling across the golden sands. Shreds of curtain material hang limply from windows and patio doors, lifting and dropping in the occasional breeze.

You hear some girls screaming, and look round to see a group of boys soaking them with water bottles, laughing when the girls scramble to their feet and retaliate with flat stinging hands. The sounds carry softly across the water.

You'd seen a map, this morning, at the entrance to the city walls, marked with clusters of red dots. The red dots were to show where mortar shells had landed during the war, where fires had started, where roofs had come crashing in. It was the only sign you could see, at first, that anything had happened here. Everything in the town seemed neat and clean and smooth: the streets polished to a shine, the ancient stonework unaffected by the destruction which had so recently poured down upon it. But when you'd looked closer you'd seen that the famous handmade roof tiles had been outnumbered by replacements in a uniform orange red, and that the stonework of the historic city walls alternated between a weathered grey and the hard white gleam of something new. There were whole streets boarded off from the public, piled with rubble. There were buildings whose front-ages had been cleaned and repaired but which were still gutted behind the shutters. And in a tiny courtyard work-shop, under the shade of a tall lemon tree, you'd seen a fat-shouldered stonemason carving replica cornices and crests, the shattered originals laid out in fragments in front of him, glancing over his shoulder as if to be sure that no one could see. You'd wondered how long it would take for this rebuilding to be complete. How much longer it would take for the new stones to look anything like the old.

The others are halfway up the hill now, walking slowly along the pine-needled path, letting their hands trail through the sweet-smelling bushes, stopping for a drink of water and looking down at the calm shining sea. You watch them for a moment. You wave, but none of them sees. You call. If you were to get out now you might be able to catch up with them before they get on the bus. But if you wait for the next bus, they'll have cleared up by the time you get back, and got some food ready, and be waiting for you. Jo went out to the market before lunch, so the apartment's small kitchen is well stocked. You can imagine arriving back to find the others sitting on the terrace around a table loaded with food: bread and cheese and oranges, olives and pickles and jam, big packets of paprika-flavoured crisps. You can imagine cracking open a beer and joining them, making plans for the night.

You turn your face into the water for one more look before you get out, sucking in warm air through the snorkel. You catch sight of a larger fish than the ones you've seen so far. Something silver-blue, twice the length of your hand, drifting slowly between the rocks. It flicks its tail and glides away, and you push back with your legs to glide after it, trying not to splash. It slows again, leaning down to nibble at the wavering tips of seaweed, and as it flicks into another glide you follow, watching from above, quietly kicking your legs to keep pace.

And you think about last night. About what might have happened with Jo. Walking between the café and the bus stop, the alleys crowded, the buildings still giving out the heat of the day, the dark sky overhead squeezed between window-boxes and washing lines and women leaning out to smoke and look down at the crowds below. You lost sight of the others for a while, and then Jo was there, saying something, touching two fingers against your chest, letting one finger catch in the opening of your shirt. What did she say? It could have been nothing. The whole thing might have been nothing. But there were her fingers against your chest. That smile and turn. Walking behind her, and all the side-alleys and courtyards that might have been ducked into. And then catching up with the others at the bus stop, and nothing more being said.

You watch the fish flick its tail beneath you, stopping and starting through the sea-grass, and you curl your body across the surface to keep pace, the sun hot and sore across your back.

It happened once, last year, at a party after the exams. In the back garden, kissing against the wall of the house, and for what must have been only a few minutes there was nothing but the taste of her mouth, the movements of her hands, the press of her body. And then she'd stopped, and kissed you on the cheek, and walked unsteadily into the house, and nothing had been said about it since. It might have been nothing.

The soft wet bite of her lips, the trace of her fingers, the thin material of her skirt in your hand, the weight of her warmth against you. It was probably nothing at all.

You look up out of the water, turning to see if she's reached the top of the path. Maybe she'll hang back and wait. You're further out than you realised. It would be good to head back now, to pull yourself up on to the concrete ledge, let the sun dry the water from your back while you gather your things together and hurry along the path to join the others. You pull your arms through the water, feeling the pleasant stretch of the muscles across your shoulders and back. You kick with your legs, hard, and your feet and shins slap against the surface, and you realise how long it's been since you last swam properly like this, actually covering a distance. You should do it more often, you think, stopping for a moment to tuck the snorkel into the headband of your mask, spitting out a mouthful of seawater. You launch off again, enjoying the way your body cuts through the water, the air on your back, the sea sliding across your skin. The snorkel slips out of place, spilling water into your mouth, and you have to stop again, coughing, to clear it from your throat.

You see the others on the path, and you see a bus passing along the road, and you see the birds hanging in the warm air rising up against the side of the hill.

You take off the snorkel and mask. They're getting in the way, and you'll get back to the steps quicker without them strapped to your face. You try swimming with them held in one hand, but they slap and splash against the surface and drag you down, and you're not getting anywhere like that so you stop and tread water for a moment. You're further out than you thought.

The afternoon's quieter now. No one's jumped from the outcrop for a while. The teenagers on the ledge have started to gather their things together and drift back up the long twisting path to the road. The girl reading a book on the other bathing jetty has gone. The back of your neck feels as though it might be starting to burn. It probably would be good, after all, to catch the bus with the others. You think about just dumping the snorkel and mask, but it seems a bit over the top. There's nothing like that happening here. There's no problem. You can't be more than a hundred, maybe a hundred and fifty yards from the shore. You tie them to the drawstring of your swimming shorts instead, and swim on.

This morning, in the old town, ducking into an art gallery to escape the glaring heat, you'd found the city's war memorial, unmarked on the tourist maps. It had looked like another room of the gallery at first, and you'd drifted into the circular space expecting more vividly coloured paintings of wheat fields and birch woods and simple peasant-folk labouring over ploughs. But there were no paintings, only photographs. Black and white photographs from ceiling to floor. Row after row of young faces with dated haircuts, thin moustaches, leather jackets and striped tracksuit tops. The photos were blown up to more than life-size, and one or two had the inky smudge of a pass-port stamp circled across them. There were names, and dates, and ages: twenty-two, fifty-seven, fifteen, nine-teen, thirty-one. There were candles burning on a table in the middle of the room, a bouquet of flowers, a ragged flag. Some of the boys in the photographs had looked the same age, and had the same features, as these teenag-ers jumping from rocks and squirting water at girls, boys who would have been half the age they are now when the war happened. You wonder if any of them lost older brothers, cousins, uncles, fathers. You wonder whether any of them remember much about it; if they duck into that cool, white-washed room every now and again to remind themselves, or if they prefer instead to leap from high rocks into the warm ocean, to ride motor scooters with the sun browning their bare chests, to lie with long-limbed girls in the scented shade of aged and twisting trees.

Perhaps when you get back no one will want to go to the trouble of laying the food out on the terrace and clearing it all away again. Perhaps you'll all go to the pizzeria down by the dockside and sit at a table on the street, picking the labels off cold bottles of beer while you watch the old women offering accommodation to the tourists coming off the boats. Perhaps Jo will catch your eye and keep you talking until the others have moved on, and shift her chair so that her leg touches yours.

Swimming with the mask and snorkel tied to your shorts is worse than holding them. They're dragging out between your legs like an anchor, pulling you back. You stop and tread water again, breathing heavily. You only paid a few pounds for them. They can go. You can always tell the others you left them behind by mistake. You unpick the knots and let them fall away. They hang in the water for a moment, lifting and turning in the current. You watch them sink out of view, and realise you can't see the bottom.

The others are at the top of the path now, and one of them leans out to look down at the ledge where your things are still gathered in a heap. You wave, but whoever it is turns away and steps through the gap in the railings, crossing the road to join the others at the bus stop, out of sight.

You take a breath and swim, fiercely, lunging through the water, blinking against the salt sting, heaving for air, and there's a feeling running up and down the backs of your legs like the muscles being stretched tight but you keep swimming because you'll be there soon, climbing out, pulling yourself back on to solid ground, and you

keep swimming because there's a chance that the current
has been pushing you away from the shore, and you keep
swimming because this isn't the sort of thing that happens
to someone like you, you're a good swimmer, you're
young, and healthy, and the rocks aren't really all that
far away and it shouldn't take long to get there and there
isn't anything else you can do but now there's a pounding
sensation in your head and a reddish blur in your eyes and
a heavy pain in your chest as though the weight of all that
water is pressing against your lungs and you can't take in
enough air and so you stop again, for a moment, just to
catch your breath.

One of the boys, in the memorial photographs, had had
a look in his eyes. Startled. As though the flash of the
camera had taken him by surprise. As though he had
known what was coming. The plaque said he was seventeen. You wondered what had happened. If he really
had seen it coming. You've seen pictures of an old fort on
a nearby island, the walls spotted with bullet marks, the
entrances surrounded by shallow craters, and you imagined that boy crouching on the roof, or in the shaded
interior, holding an old rifle in his shaking hands, listening
to the encircling approach of men and equipment through
the trees and bushes outside. You imagined him listening
to their taunts. Wiping the sweat from his eyes. Avoiding the glances of the men left with him. Wondering
how they had all ended up in that place, what they could
have done to avoid it, what they were going to do now.
Knowing there was nothing they could do.

A bus stops on the road at the top of the hill. The others
must be getting on it by now, rummaging in their pockets
for change and wondering how much longer you're going

to be. When you get back they'll all be sitting out on the terrace, watching the yachts gathering in the harbour for the evening, listening to children playing up and down the back streets behind the apartment. You'll take a beer from the fridge, hold the cold wet glass against the back of your sunburnt neck, and ask where the bottle-opener is. No one will be able to find it at first, and then it will turn up, under a book or a leaflet, or in the sink with some dirty plates, and you'll flip the top off the bottle and take your seat with the others.

You swim some more, and there's a feeling in your arms and legs as though the muscles have been peeled out of them, as though the bones have softened from being in the water too long, and you can't find the energy to pull yourself forward at all.

You turn on to your back for a few moments. A rest is all you need. It's been a while since you swam in open water like this, that's all. A few moments' rest and you'll be able to swim to the rocks, to the steps, and climb out. You'll be able to hang a towel over your pounding head until you get your breath back, dripping water and sweat on to the sun-bleached concrete, feeling the warm solid ground beneath you. You'll be able to gather your things and make your way along the path, pulling on your shirt as you go. And the grasshoppers will still be calling out, and the air will be thick with rosemary and pine. The sandy soil of the path will still kick up into dusty clouds around your ankles. Your swimming trunks will be dry by the time you get to the top of the hill, and you won't have to wait long for a bus. And while you stand there the sea will be as calm and blue as ever when you look down over it, drifting out to the horizon, reaching around to other bays, other beaches, other villages and towns, other swimmers launching out into its warm and gentle embrace.

And this will be a story to tell when you get back home, sitting under the patio heaters at the Golf Club bar, looking out over the cold North Sea and saying it was a nice holiday but I nearly never made it home. Or later this evening, sitting at some pavement cafe in a noisy bustling square with tall glasses of cold beer, telling the story of how you'd almost swum out too far. How you'd had to dump the snorkel and mask. It was a close one, you'll tell them. I called out but you didn't hear. No one heard. Best be more careful next time, someone will probably say; even when the water looks calm there are still currents. Just because it's warmer than back home doesn't mean you can treat it like a swimming pool, they'll say, and you'll laugh and say, well, I know that now. And everyone will go quiet for a moment, thinking about it, until the waiter comes past and you order another round of drinks. And raise a silent toast to all the good things. The cold wet glass against the back of your sunburnt neck. The trace of her fingers, the soft wet bite of her lips. The juice of an orange spilling down your chin. Music, and dancing, and voices colliding in the warm night air.

You swim, and you rest. It won't take long now. It's not too far. You look up, past the headland and into the next bay along, and you swim and you rest a little more. Sometimes it happens like this.

JEANETTE WINTERSON

All I Know About Gertrude Stein

In 1907 a woman from San Francisco named Alice B. Toklas arrived in Paris. She was going to meet a fellow American living there already. She was excited because she'd heard a lot about Gertrude Stein.

IN 2011 a woman from London named Louise was travelling by Eurostar to Paris. Louise was troubled. Louise was travelling alone because she was trying to understand something about love.

Louise was in a relationship; it felt like a ship, though her vessel was a small boat rowed by herself with a cabin for her lover. Her lover's ship was much bigger and carried crew and passengers. There was always a party going on. Her lover was at the centre of a busy world. Louise was her own world; self-contained, solitary, intense. She did not know how to reconcile these opposites – if opposites they were – and to make things more complicated, it was Louise who wanted the two of them to live together. Her lover said no – they were good as they were – and the solitary Louise and the sociable lover could not be in the same boat.

And so Louise was travelling alone to Paris.

I am Louise.

I took the Metro to Cité. I walked past Notre-Dame and thought of the hunchback Quasimodo swinging his mis-shapen body across the bell-ropes of love for Esmeralda. Quasimodo was a deaf mute. Cupid is blind. Freud called love an 'overestimation of the object'. But I would swing through the ringing world for you.

Alice Toklas had no previous experience of love. Her mother died young – young for the mother and young for Alice – and Alice played the piano and kept house for her father and brothers. She ordered the meat, managed the budget, supervised the kitchen. And then she came to Paris and met Gertrude Stein.

Gertrude Stein's mother died young too – and you never fully recover from that – actually you never recover at all; you take it with you as an open wound – but with luck that is not the end of the story.

Gertrude had a modest but sufficient private income. She and her brother Leo had long since left the USA to set up house in Paris in the rue de Fleurus. Gertrude wrote. Leo painted. They bought modern art. They bought Matisse when no one did and they bought Picasso when no one did. Pablo and Gertrude became great friends.

But Gertrude was lonely. Gertrude was a writer. Gertrude was lonely.

I find myself returning again and again to the same familiar condition of solitariness. Is it sex that makes this happen? If it were not for sex, wouldn't we each be content with our friends, their companionship and confidences? I love my friends. I am a good friend. But with my lover I begin to feel alone.

A friend of mine can be happy without a lover; she will have an affair if she wants one, but she doesn't take the trouble to love.

I do very badly without a lover. I pine, I sigh, I sleep, I dream, I set the table for two and stare into the empty chair. I could invite a friend – sometimes I do – but that is not the point; the point is that I am always wondering where you are even when you don't exist.

Sometimes I have affairs. But though I enjoy the bed, I feel angry at the fraud; the closeness without the cost.

I know what the cost is: the more I love you, the more I feel alone.

On 23 May 1907 Gertrude Stein met Alice B. Toklas. Gertrude: fat, sexy, genial, powerful. Alice: a tiny unicorn, nervous, clever, watchful, determined. When Gertrude opened the door to the atelier of 27 rue de Fleurus, Alice tried to sit down but couldn't, because the chairs were Stein-size and Alice was Toklas-size and her feet did not reach the floor.

'The world keeps turning round and round,' said Gertrude, 'but you have to sit somewhere.'

I sat opposite you and I liked your dishevelled look; hair in your eyes and your clothes a strategic mess. We were both survivors of other shipwrecks. You looked sad. I wanted to see you again.

For a while we corresponded by email, charming each other in fonts and pixels. Did you . . . do you . . . would you like to . . . I wonder if . . .

Every day Miss Toklas sent a petit bleu to Miss Stein to arrange a walk in the Luxembourg Gardens or a visit to a bookshop or to look at pictures. One day Alice was late. Gertrude was so angry. Alice picked up her gloves to leave but as she was walking across the courtyard Gertrude called out, 'It is not too late to go for a walk.'

We went walking on Hampstead Heath. We walked for two hours straight ahead going round in circles. The circles were the two compass-turns of your desire and mine. The overlap is where we kissed.

The Stein and Toklas love affair was about sex.

They went on holiday together – the dripping heat of Italy and Gertrude liking to walk in the noonday sun.

They talked about *The Taming of the Shrew* – that play by Shakespeare – the one where Petruchio breaks Kate into loving him – a strange play. Not a poster-play for feminism.

GERTRUDE: A wife hangs upon her husband – that is what Shakespeare says.

ALICE: But you have never married.

GERTRUDE: I would like a wife.

ALICE: What kind of a wife would she be?

GERTRUDE: Ardent, able, clever, present. Yes, very present.

ALICE: I am going back to San Francisco in ten days.

GERTRUDE: I have enjoyed your visits every day to the rue de Fleurus . . . And they walked in silence up the hill into the crest of the sun and Alice began to shed her clothes – her stockings, her cherry-red corset. Alice began to undress the past. At the top of the hill they sat down and Gertrude did not look at her.

GERTRUDE: When all is said one is wedded to bed.

It was the beginning of their love affair.

I met my lover two years ago and I fell in love. I fell like a stray star caught in the orbit of Venus. Love had me. Love held me. Love like wrist-cords. Love like a voice from a long way off. I love your voice on the phone.

Below me on the *quai* there's a skinny boy singing to his guitar: 'All You Need is Love'. Couples holding hands throw him coins because they want to believe that it is true. They want to believe that they are true.

But the love question is harder to solve than the Grand Unified Theory of Everything.

If you were Dante you'd say they were the same thing – 'the love that moves the sun and the other stars'.

But love is in trouble.

Women used to be in charge of love – it was our whole domain, the business of our lives, to give love to make love to mend love to tend love.

Men needed women to be love so that men could do all the things you can't do without love – but no one acknowledged the secret necessity of love. Except in those dedications: To My Wife.

Now we have our own money and we can vote. We are career-women. (No such word as career-man.) We are more than the love interest. More than love. We are independent. Equal.

But . . . What happened to love?

We were confident that love would always be there, like air, like water, like summer, like sun. Love could take care of itself. We didn't notice the quiet tending of love, the small daily repairs to the fabric of love. The faithful gigantic work that kept love as regular as light.

Love is an ecosystem like any other. You can't drain it and strip-mine it, drill it and build over it and wonder where the birds and the bees have gone. Love is where we want to live. Planet Love.

When we met, the most surprising and touching thing to me was that you always answered your phone when I called. You were not too important to be available. You are important but you recognised love as more important.

I started to believe you. I started to believe in you. Love has a religious quality to it – it depends on the unseen and it makes miracles out of itself. And there is always a sacrifice. I don't think we talk about love in real terms any more. We talk about partnership. We talk about romance. We talk about sex. We talk about divorce. I don't think we talk about love at all.

Alice Toklas never went back to San Francisco. She never saw her family again. Gertrude's brother Leo soon moved out of the rue de Fleurus and Alice moved in. They were together every day for the next forty years. Shall I write that again? *They were together every day for the next forty years* . . . And they never stopped having sex.

Gertrude Stein liked giving Alice an orgasm – she called it 'making a cow come out'. Nobody knows why – unless Alice made *moo* noises when she hit it. Gertrude said, 'I am the best cow-giver in the world.' Gertrude Stein liked repetition too – of verbs and words and orgasms.

We love the habits of love. The way you wear your hair. The way you drink your coffee. The way you turn your back on me in the mornings so that I will shift to fit myself round you. The way you open the door when you see me coming home. When I leave I look up at the window and I know you will be watching me, watching over me go.

And at the same time love needs to be new every day. The fresh damp risen-up feel of love.

Gertrude Stein said – *There is no there there* – at once refusing materiality and consolation.

I am lonely when I love because I feel the immensity of the task – the stoking and tending of love. I feel unable, overwhelmed. I feel I can only fail. So I hide and I cling all at once. I need you near me, in my house, but I don't want you to find my hiding place. Hold me. Don't come too close.

I decided to walk to the Musée Picasso because the Picasso portrait of Gertrude Stein was on loan there from the Metropolitan Museum of Art, New York. It is a famous picture. Gertrude is massy in the frame, her head almost a kabuki mask. It doesn't look like her but it couldn't be anyone else. Picasso took ninety sittings to paint it and couldn't get the head right. Gertrude said, *'Paint it out and paint it in when I am not there.'*

Picasso did that and Gertrude was very pleased. She hung the picture over her fireplace, and during the Second World War she and Alice took it to the countryside for five years, wrapped in a sheet, in their old open-topped Ford.

Gertrude said to Picasso, *'Paint what is really there. Not what you can see, but what is really there.'*

How can I trust myself like that? To see through the screens that shield me from love and not be so afraid of what I see that I break up, break off, or settle for the diluted version?

I have done all those things before.

And when I am not doing those things I am telling myself that I am an independent woman who should not be limited by/to love.

But love has no limits. Love seems to be a continuous

condition like the universe. But the universe is remote except for this planet we call home, and love means nothing unless it is real and in our hands.

Give me your hand.

There's a school party at the museum. They are not looking at Picasso; they are giggling over an iPhone. Poor kids, they're all on Facebook posting themselves at a party. They are all having sex all the time because fucking is the new frigid. Look at their Facebook faces, defiant, unhappy. The F-words. Facebook, fucking, frigid, faking it.

Gertrude Stein called the generation between the wars 'the lost generation'. We are the upgrade generation. Get a new model; phone girlfriend car. Gertrude Stein hated commas. You can see why when car phone girlfriend are the same and interchangeable. Why would I work with love when I can replace the object of love?

Men still trade in their women – nothing feminism can do about that. Now women trade in themselves – new breasts, new face, new body. What will happen to these girls giggling over their iPhones?

They are the upload generation. Neophytes in the service of the savage god of the social network.

Fear. F is for fear.

In this bleak and broken world, what chance is there for love? Love is dating sites and bytes of love. Love is a stream of body parts. But if we part, I want to know that love had time enough. It takes a long time to be close to you.

Gertrude Stein could not be rushed, although she did not like to be kept waiting. Her time was her own. She had a big white poodle called Basket and she walked herself and her poodle round Paris.

Sometimes Basket went in the car with Gertrude and Alice and Alice went into the shops – and she liked that – and Gertrude stayed in the car – and she liked that. She wrote things in her notebook. She wrote every day but only for half an hour.

'*It takes a lot of time to write for half an hour,*' said Gertrude.

She wrote unpublished for thirty years. And then, in 1934, written in six weeks, *The Autobiography of Alice B. Toklas* by Gertrude Stein became a huge best-seller. Gertrude and Alice boarded the SS *Champion* and sailed for New York. Alice got a fur coat. Gertrude got a leopard-skin cap. Their travelling suits were made by Pierre Balmain. He was just a boy in those days.

When they and their outfits arrived in New York City, the ticker tape in Times Square tweeted:

GERTRUDE STEIN HAS LANDED IN NEW YORK.

'*As if we did not know it . . .*' said Alice.

The pressmen surrounded the Algonquin Hotel. The vendors selling frankfurters and pretzels watched from across the street.

VENDOR 1: The fat one built like a boulder, that's Gertrude Stein.

VENDOR 2: The thin one cut like a chisel . . .

VENDOR 1: That's Alice B. Toklas.

The press bulbs flashed like they were movie stars.

PRESSMAN: Hey, Miss Stein, why don't you write the way you talk? (Laughter.)

GERTRUDE: Why don't you read the way I write?

Everyone is laughing. Gertrude loves fame. Fame loves Gertrude.

VENDOR 2: Where's the husbands?

VENDOR 1: They got no husbands. (He passes a frankfurter through a pretzel and nods significantly.)

VENDOR 2: (low whistle) No kidding? But ain't they American gals?

VENDOR 1: Sure, but they been living in Paris.

Living with you would be the ultimate romance. I am a romantic and that is my defence against the love-commodity. I can't buy love but I don't want to rent it either. I would like to find a way to make the days with you be ours. I would like to bring my bag and unpack it.

You say we will fail, get frustrated, fall out, fight. All the F-words.

But there is another one: forgive.

In 1946 Gertrude Stein was suddenly admitted to the American Hospital at Neuilly. She had stomach cancer.

Only a few months earlier they had come back to Paris, in 1945 – the war over at last – to find the seal of the Gestapo on their apartment. Their silver and linen had been taken and the pictures were packed up ready to be removed to German art collections – that's what happened if you were a Jew.

Alice had been so upset, but Gertrude wanted to get her portrait by Picasso hung over the fireplace again, sit down in their two armchairs either side of the fire, and have some tea.

'The apartment is here. You are here. I am here,' she said.

At the hospital the doctor came into the room. They administered the anaesthetic. Gertrude had been advised against an operation but she did not believe in death – at least not for her. She did not believe in the afterlife either. There was no *there there*. Everything was *here*. Gertrude Stein was present tense.

She held Alice's hand. She said to Alice, *What is the answer?* But Alice was crying and only shook her head. Gertrude laughed her big rich laugh. 'Then what is the question?'

The trolley bearing Gertrude was wheeled away. Alice walked beside her lover as though she were walking beside her whole life. Gertrude never came back.

The question is: How do we love?

It is a personal question each to each, intense, private, frightening, necessary. It is a world question too, angry, refusing, demanding, difficult.

Love is not sentimental. Love is not second best.

Women will have to take up arms for love.

Take me in your arms. This is the Here that we have.

MICHAEL MARSHALL SMITH

Sad, Dark Thing

AIMLESS. A SHORT, simple word. It means 'without aim', where 'aim' derives from the idea of calculation with a view to action. Without purpose or direction, therefore, without a considered goal or future that you can see. People mainly use the word in a blunt, softened fashion. They walk 'aimlessly' down a street, not sure whether to have a coffee or if they should they check out the new magazines in the bookstore or maybe sit on that bench and watch the world go by. It's not a big deal, this aimlessness. It's a temporary state and often comes with a side order of ease. An hour without something hanging over you, with no great need to do or achieve anything in particular? In this world of busy lives and do-this and do-that, it sounds pretty good.

But being wholly without purpose? With no direction home? That is not such a good deal. Being truly aimless is like being dead. It may even be the same thing, or worse. It is the aimless who find the wrong roads, and go down them, simply because they have nowhere else to go.

Miller usually found himself driving on Saturday afternoons. He could make the morning go away by staying in bed an extra half-hour, tidying away stray emails, spending time on the deck, looking out over the forest with a magazine or the iPad and a succession of coffees. He made the coffees in a machine that sat on the kitchen counter and cost nearly eight hundred dollars. It made a very good cup of coffee. It should. It had cost nearly eight hundred dollars.

By noon a combination of caffeine and other factors would mean that he wasn't very hungry. He would go back indoors nonetheless, and put together a plate from the fridge. The ingredients would be things he'd gathered from delis up in San Francisco during the week, or else from the New Leaf markets in Santa Cruz or Felton as he returned home on Friday afternoon. The idea was that this would constitute a treat, and remind him of the good things in life. That was the idea. He would also pour some juice into one of the only two glasses in the cabinet that got any use. The other was his scotch glass, the one with the faded white logo on it, but that only came out in the evenings. He was very firm about that.

He would bring the plate and glass back out and eat at the table which stood further along the deck from the chair in which he'd spent most of the morning. By then the sun would have moved around, and the table got shade, which he preferred when he was eating. The change in position was also supposed to make it feel like he was doing something different to what he'd done all morning, though it did not, especially. He was still a man sitting in silence on a raised deck, within view of many trees, eating expensive foods that tasted like cardboard.

Afterward he took the plate indoors and washed it in the sink. He had a dishwasher, naturally. Dishwashers are there to save time. He washed the plate and silverware by hand, watching the water swirl away and then drying everything and putting it to one side. He was down a wife, and a child, now living three hundred miles away. He was short on women and children, therefore, but in their place, from the hollows they had left behind, he had time. Time crawled in an endless parade of minutes from between those cracks, arriving like an army of little black ants, crawling up over his skin, up his face, and into his mouth, ears and eyes.

So why not wash the plate. And the knife, and the fork, and the glass. Hold back the ants, for a few minutes, at least.

He never left the house with a goal. On those afternoons he was, truly, aimless. From where the house stood, high in the Santa Cruz mountains, he could have reached a number of diverting places within an hour or two. San Jose. Saratoga. Los Gatos. Santa Cruz itself, then south to Monterey, Carmel and Big Sur. Even way down to Los Angeles, if he felt like making a weekend of it.

And then what?

Instead he simply drove.

There are only so many major routes you can take through the area's mountains and redwood forests. Highways 17 and 9, or the road out over to Bonny Doon, Route 1 north or south. Of these, only 17 is of any real size. In between the main thoroughfares, however, there are other options. Roads that don't do much except connect one minor two-lane highway to another. Roads that used to count for something before modern alternatives came along to supplant or supersede or negate them.

Side roads, old roads, forgotten roads.

Usually there wasn't much to see down these last roads. Stretches of forest, maybe a stream, eventually a house, well back from the road. Rural, mountainous backwoods where the tree and poison oak reigned supreme. Chains

across tracks which led down or up into the woods, some
gentle inclines, others pretty steep, meandering off toward
some house which stood even further from the through-
lines, back in a twenty- or fifty-acre lot. Every now and
then you'd pass one of the area's very few tourist traps,
like the 'Mystery Spot', an old-fashioned affair which
claimed to honour a site of 'Unfathomable Weirdness' but
in fact paid cheerful homage to geometry, and to man's
willingness to be deceived.

He'd seen all of these long ago. The local attractions
with his wife and child, the shadowed roads and tracks on
his own solitary excursions over the last few months. At
least, you might have thought he would have seen them
all. Every Saturday he drove, however, and every time he
found a road he had never seen before.

Today the road was off Branciforte Drive, the long, old
highway which heads off through largely uncolonised
regions of the mountains and forests to the south-east of
Scott's Valley. As he drove north along it, mind elsewhere
and nowhere, he noticed a turning. A glance in the rear-
view mirror showed no one behind and so he slowed to
peer along the turn.

A two-lane road, overhung with tall trees, including
some redwoods. It gave no indication of leading anywhere at all.

Fine by him.

He made the turn and drove on. The trees were tall
and thick, cutting off much of the light from above. The
road passed smoothly up and down, riding the natural
contours, curving abruptly once in a while to avoid the
trunk of an especially big tree or to skirt a small canyon
carved out over millennia by some small and bloody-
minded stream. There were no houses or other signs of

habitation. Could be public land, he was beginning to think, though he didn't recall there being any around here and hadn't seen any indication of a park boundary, and then he saw a sign by the road up ahead.

STOP

That's all it said. Despite himself, he found he was doing just that, pulling over toward it. When the car was stationary, he looked at the sign curiously. It had been hand-lettered, some time ago, in black marker on a panel cut from a cardboard box and nailed to a tree.

He looked back the way he'd come, and then up the road once more. He saw no traffic in either direction, and also no indication of why the sign would be here. Sure, the road curved again about forty yards ahead, but no more markedly than it had ten or fifteen times since he'd left Branciforte Drive. There had been no warning signs on those bends. If you simply wanted to people to observe the speed limit then you'd be more likely to advise them to 'Slow', and anyway it didn't look at all like an official sign.

Then he realised that, further on, there was in fact a turning off the road.

He took his foot off the brake and let the car roll forward down the slope, crunching over twigs and gravel. A driveway, it looked like, though a long one, bending off into the trees. Single lane, roughly made up. Maybe five yards down it was another sign, evidently the work of the same craftsman as the previous.

TOURISTS WELCOME

He grunted, in something like a laugh. If you had yourself some kind of attraction, of course tourists were welcome. What would be the point otherwise? It was a strange way of putting it.

An odd way of advertising it, too. No indication of

what was in store or why a busy family should turn off what was already a pretty minor road and head off into the woods. No lure except those two words.

They were working on him, though, he had to admit. He eased his foot gently back on the gas and carefully directed the car along the track, between the trees.

After about a quarter of a mile he saw a building ahead. A couple of them, in fact, arranged in a loose compound. One a ramshackle two-storey farmhouse, the other a disused barn. There was also something that was or had been a garage, with a broken-down truck/tractor parked diagonally in front of it. It was parked insofar as it was not moving, at least, not in the sense that whoever had last driven the thing had made any effort, when abandoning it, to align its form with anything. The surfaces of the vehicle were dusty and rusted and liberally covered in old leaves and specks of bark. A wooden crate, about four feet square, stood rotting in the back. The near front tyre was flat.

The track ended in a widened parking area, big enough for four or five cars. It was empty. There was no sign of life at all, in fact, but something – he wasn't sure what – said this habitation was a going concern, rather than collection of ruins that someone had walked away from at some point in the last few years.

Nailed to a tree in front of the main house, was another cardboard sign.

WELCOME

He parked, turned off the engine, and got out. It was very quiet. It usually is in those mountains, when you're away from the road. Sometimes you'll hear the faint roar of an airplane, way up above, but apart from that it's just the occasional tweet of some winged creature or an indistinct rustle as something small and furry or scaly makes its way through the bushes.

He stood for a few minutes, flapping his hand to discourage a noisy fly which appeared from nowhere, bothered his face, and then zipped chaotically off.

Eventually he called out. 'Hello?'

You'd think that – on what was evidently a very slow day for this attraction, whatever it was – the sound of an arriving vehicle would have someone bustling into sight, eager to make a few bucks, to pitch their wares. He stood a few minutes more, however, without seeing or hearing any sign of life. It figured. Aimless people find aimless things, and it didn't seem like much was going to happen here. You find what you're looking for, and he hadn't been looking for anything at all.

He turned back toward the car, aware that he wasn't even feeling disappointment. He hadn't expected much, and that's exactly what he'd got.

As he held up his hand to press the button to unlock the doors, however, he heard a creaking sound.

He turned back to see there was now a man on the tilting porch that ran along half of the front of the wooden house. He was dressed in canvas jeans and a vest that had probably once been white. The man had probably once been clean, too, though he looked now like he'd spent most of the morning trying to fix the underside of a car. Perhaps he had.

'What you want?'

His voice was flat and unwelcoming. He looked to be in his mid to late fifties. Hair once black was now half grey, and also none too clean. He did not look like he'd been either expecting or desirous of company.

'What have you got?'

The man on the porch leant on the rail and kept looking at him, but said nothing.

'It says "Tourists Welcome",' Miller said, when it became clear the local had nothing to offer. 'I'm not feeling especially welcome, to be honest.'

The man on the porch looked weary. 'Christ. The boy was supposed to take down those damned signs. They still up?'

'Yes.'

'Even the one out on the road, says "Stop"?'

'Yes,' Miller said. 'Otherwise I wouldn't have stopped.'

The other man swore and shook his head. 'Told the boy weeks ago. Told him I don't know how many times.'

Miller frowned. 'You don't notice, when you drive in and out? That the signs are still there?'

'Haven't been to town in a while.'

'Well, look. I turned down your road because it looked like there was something to see.'

'Nope. Doesn't say anything like that.'

'It's implied, though, wouldn't you say?'

The man lifted his chin a little. 'You a lawyer?'

'No. I'm a businessman. With time on my hands. Is there something to see here, or not?'

After a moment the man on the porch straightened, and came walking down the steps.

'One dollar,' he said. 'As you're here.'

'For what? The parking?'

The man stared at him as if he was crazy. 'No. To see.'

'One dollar?' It seemed inconceivable that in this day and age there would be anything under the sun for a dollar, especially if it was trying to present as something worth experiencing. 'Really?'

'That's cheap,' the man said, misunderstanding.

'It is what it is,' Miller said, getting his wallet out and pulling a dollar bill from it.

The other man laughed, a short, sour sound. 'You got that right.'

After he'd taken the dollar and stuffed it into one of the pockets of his jeans, the man walked away. Miller took this to mean that he should follow, and so he did. It looked for a moment as if they were headed toward the house, but then the path – such as it was – took an abrupt right onto a course that led them between the house and the tilting barn. The house was large and gabled, and must once have been quite something. Lord knows what it was doing out here, lost by itself in a patch of forest that had never been near a major road or town or anyplace else that people with money might wish to be. Its glory days were long behind it, anyway. Looking up at it, you'd give it about another five years standing, unless someone got onto rebuilding or at least shoring it right away.

The man led the way through slender trunks into an area around the back of the barn. Though the land in front of the house and around the side had barely been what you'd think of as tamed, here the forest abruptly came into its own. Trees of significant size shot up all around, looking – as redwoods do – like they'd been there since the dawn of time. A sharp, rocky incline led down toward a stream about thirty yards away. The stream was perhaps eight feet across, with steep sides. A rickety bridge of old, grey wood lay across it. The man led him to the near side of this, and then stopped.

'What?'

'This is it.'

Miller looked again at the bridge. 'A dollar, to look at

a bridge some guy threw up fifty years ago?' Suddenly it
wasn't seeming so dumb a pricing system after all.

The man handed him a small, tarnished key, and raised
his other arm to point. Between the trees on the other side
of the creek was a small hut.

'It's in there.'

'What is?'

The man shrugged. 'A sad, dark thing.'

The water which trickled below the bridge smelt fresh
and clean. Miller got a better look at the hut, shed, whatever, when he reached the other side. It was about half
the size of a log cabin, but made of grey, battered planks
instead of logs. The patterns of lichen over the sides and
the moss-covered roof said it been here, and in this form,
for a good long time – far longer than the house, most
likely. Could be an original settler's cabin, the home of
whichever long-ago pioneer had first arrived here, driven
west by hope or desperation. It looked about contemporary with the rickety bridge, certainly.

There was a small padlock on the door.

He looked back.

The other man was still standing at the far end of the
bridge, looking up at the canopy of leaves above. It wasn't
clear what he'd be looking at, but it didn't seem like he
was waiting for the right moment to rush over, bang the
other guy on the head, and steal his wallet. If he'd wanted
to do that he could have done it back up at the house.
There was no sign of anyone else around – this boy he'd
mentioned, for example – and he looked like he was
waiting patiently for the conclusion of whatever needed
to happen for him to have earned his dollar.

Miller turned back and fitted the key in the lock. It was
stiff, but it turned. He opened the door. Inside was total

dark. He hesitated, looked back across the bridge, but the man had gone.

He opened the door further, and stepped inside.

The interior of the cabin was cooler than it had been outside, but also stuffy. There was a faint smell. Not a bad smell, particularly. It was like old, damp leaves. It was like the back of a closet where you store things you do not need. It was like a corner of the attic of a house not much loved, in the night, after rain.

The only light was that which managed to get past him from the door behind. The cabin had no windows, or if it had, they had been covered over. The door he'd entered by was right at one end of the building, which meant the rest of the interior led ahead. It could only have been ten, twelve feet. It seemed longer, because it was so dark. The man stood there, not sure what happened next.

The door slowly swung closed behind him, not all the way, but leaving a gap of a couple of inches. No-one came and shut it on him or turned the lock or started hollering about he'd have to pay a thousand bucks to get back out again. The man waited.

In a while, there was a quiet sound.

It was a rustling. Not quite a shuffling. A sense of something moving a little at the far end, turning away from the wall, perhaps. Just after the sound, there was a low waft of a new odour, as if the movement had caused something to change its relationship to the environment, as if a body long held curled or crouched in a particular shape or position had realigned enough for hidden sweat to be released into the unmoving air.

Miller froze.

In all his life, he'd never felt the hairs on the back of his neck rise. You read about it, hear about it. You knew they were supposed to do it, but he'd never felt it, not his own hairs, on his own neck. They did it then, though, and the peculiar thing was that he was not afraid, or not only that.

He was in there with something, that was for certain. It was not a known thing, either. It was . . . he didn't know. He wasn't sure. He just knew that there was something over there in the darkness. Something about the size of a man, he thought, maybe a little smaller.

He wasn't sure it was male, though. Something said to him it was female. He couldn't imagine where this impression might be coming from, as he couldn't see it and he couldn't hear anything, either – after the initial movement, it had been still. There was just something in the air that told him things about it, that said underneath the shadows it wrapped around itself like a pair of dark angel's wings, it knew despair, bitter madness and melancholy better even than he did. He knew that beneath those shadows it was naked, and not male.

He knew also that it was this, and not fear, that was making his breathing come ragged and forced.

He stayed in there with it for half an hour, doing nothing, just listening, staring into the darkness but not seeing anything. That's how long it seemed like it had been, anyway, when he eventually emerged back into the forest. It was hard to tell.

He closed the cabin door behind him but he did not lock it, because he saw that the man was back, standing once more at the far end of the bridge. Miller clasped the key firmly in his fist and walked over toward him.

'How much?' he said.

'For what? You already paid.'

'No,' Miller said. 'I want to buy it.'

It was eight by the time Miller got back to his house. He didn't know how that could be unless he'd spent longer in the cabin than he realised. It didn't matter a whole lot, and in fact there were good things about it. The light had begun to fade. In twenty minutes it would be gone entirely. He spent those minutes sitting in the front seat of the car, waiting for darkness, his mind as close to a comfortable blank as it had been in a long time.

When it was finally dark he got out the car and went over to the house. He dealt with the security system, opened the front door and left it hanging open.

He walked back to the vehicle and went around to the trunk. He rested his hand on the metal there for a moment, and it felt cold. He unlocked the back and turned away, not fast but naturally, and walked toward the set of wooden steps which led to the smaller of the two raised decks. He walked up them and stood there for a few minutes, looking out into the dark stand of trees, and then turned and headed back down the steps toward the car.

The trunk was empty now, and so he shut it, and walked slowly toward the open door of his house, and went inside, and shut and locked that door behind him too.

It was night, and it was dark, and they were both inside and that felt right.

He poured a small scotch in a large glass. He took it out through the sliding glass doors to the chair on the main deck where he'd spent the morning, and sat there cradling the drink, taking a sip once in a while. He found himself remembering, as he often did at this time, the first time he'd met his wife. He'd been living down on East Cliff then, in a house which was much smaller that this one but only a couple of minutes' walk from the beach. Late one Saturday afternoon, bored and restless, he'd taken a walk to the Crow's Nest, the big restaurant that was the only place to eat or drink along that stretch. He'd bought a similar scotch at the upstairs bar and taken it out onto the balcony to watch the sun go down over the harbour. After a while he noticed that, amongst the family groups of sunburned tourists and knots of tattooed locals there was a woman sitting at a table by herself. She had a tall glass of beer and seemed to be doing the same thing he was, and he wondered why. Not why she was doing that, but why he was – why they both were. He did not know then, and he did not know now, why people sit and look out into the distance by themselves, or what they hope to see.

After a couple more drinks he went over and intro- duced himself. Her name was Catherine and she worked at the university. They got married eighteen months later and though by then – his business having taken off in the meantime – he could have afforded anywhere in town, they hired out the Crow's Nest and had the wedding party there. A year after that their daughter was born and they called her Matilde, after Catherine's mother, who was French. Business was still good and they moved out of his place on East Cliff and into the big house he had built in the mountains and for seven years all was good, and then, for some reason, it was no longer good any more. He didn't think it had been his fault, though it could have been. He didn't think it was her fault either, though that too was possible. It had simply stopped working. They'd been two people, and then one, but then two again, facing different ways. There had been a view to share together, then there was not, and if you look with only one eye then there is no depth of field. There had been no infidelity. In some ways that might have been easier. It would have been something to react to, to blame, to hide behind. Far worse, in fact, to sit on opposite sides of the breakfast table and wonder who the other person was, and why they were there, and when they would go.

Six months later, she did. Matilde went with her, of course. He didn't think there was much more that could be said or understood on the subject. When first he'd sat out on this deck alone, trying to work it all through in his head, the recounting could take hours. As time went on, the story seemed to get shorter and shorter. As they said around these parts, it is what it is.

Or it was what it was.

Time passed and then it was late. The scotch was long gone but he didn't feel the desire for any more. He took the glass indoors and washed it at the sink, putting it on the draining board next to the plate and the knife and the fork from lunch. No lights were on. He hadn't bothered to flick any switches when he came in, and – having sat for so long out on the deck – his eyes were accustomed, and he felt no need to turn any on now.

He dried his hands on a cloth and walked around the house, aimlessly at first. He had done this many times in the last few months, hearing echoes. When he got to the area which had been Catherine's study, he stopped. There was nothing left in the space now bar the empty desk and the empty bookshelves. He could tell that the chair had been moved, however. He didn't recall precisely how it had been, or when he'd last listlessly walked this way, but he knew that it had been moved, somehow.

He went back to walking, and eventually fetched up outside the room that had been Matilde's. The door was slightly ajar. The space beyond was dark.

He could feel a warmth coming out of it, though, and heard a sound in there, something quiet, and he turned and walked slowly away.

He took a shower in the dark. Afterward he padded back to the kitchen in his bare feet and a gown and picked his scotch glass up from the draining board. Even after many, many trips through the dishwasher you could see the ghost of the restaurant logo that had once been stamped on it, the remains of a mast and a crow's nest. Catherine had slipped it into her purse one long-ago night, without him knowing about it, and then given the glass to him as an anniversary present. How did a person who would do that change into the person now living half the state away? He didn't know, any more than he knew why he had so little to say on the phone to his daughter, or why people sat and looked at views, or why they drove to nowhere on Saturday afternoons. Our heads turn and point at things. Light comes into our eyes. Words come out of our mouths.

And then? And so?

Carefully, he brought the edge of the glass down upon the edge of the counter. It broke pretty much as he'd hoped it would, the base remaining in one piece, the sides shattering into several jagged points.

He padded back through into the bedroom, put the broken glass on the nightstand, took off the robe, and lay back on the bed. That's how they'd always done it, when they'd wanted to signal that tonight didn't have to just be about going to sleep. Under the covers with a book, then probably not tonight, Josephine.

Naked and on top, on the other hand . . .

A shorthand. A shared language. There is little sadder, however, than a tongue for which only one speaker remains. He closed his eyes, and after a while, for the first time since he'd stood stunned in the driveway and watched his family leave, he cried.

Afterward he lay and waited.

She came in the night.

Three days later, in the late afternoon, a battered truck pulled down into the driveway and parked alongside the car that was there. It was the first time the truck had been on the road in nearly two years, and the driver left the engine running when he got out because he wasn't all that sure it would start up again. The patched front tyre was holding up, though, for now.

He went around the back and opened up the wooden crate, propping the flap with a stick. Then he walked over to the big front door and rang on the bell. Waited a while, and did it again. No answer. Of course.

He rubbed his face in his hands, wearily, took a step back. The door looked solid. No way a kick would get it open. He looked around and saw the steps up to the side deck.

When he got around to the back of the house he picked up the chair that sat by itself, hefted it to judge the weight, and threw it through the big glass door. When he'd satisfied himself that the hole in the smashed glass was big enough, he walked back along the deck and around the front and then up the driveway to stand on the road for a while, out of view of the house.

He smoked a cigarette, and then another to be sure, and when he came back down the driveway he was relived to see that the flap on the crate on the back of his truck was now closed.

He climbed into the cab and sat a moment, looking

at the big house. Then he put the truck into reverse, got back up to the highway, and drove slowly home.

When he made the turn into his own drive later, he saw the STOP sign was still there. Didn't matter how many times he told the boy, the sign was still there.

He drove along the track to the house, parked the truck. He opened the crate without looking at it, and went inside.

Later, sitting on his porch in the darkness, he listened to the sound of the wind moving through the tops of the trees all around. He drank a warm beer, and then another. He looked at the grime on his hands. He wondered what it was that made some people catch sight of the sign, what it was in their eyes, what it was in the way they looked, that made them see. He wondered how the man in the big house had done it, and hoped he had not suffered much. He wondered why he had never attempted the same thing. He wondered why it was only on nights like these that he was able to remember that his boy had been dead twenty years.

Finally he went indoors and lay in bed staring at the ceiling. He did this every night, even though there was never anything there to see: nothing unless it is that sad, dark thing that eventually takes us in its arms and makes us sleep.

AK BENEDICT

The Last Library

T HE TOUR GUIDE clears her throat. 'The Museum of Last Things is the ultimate museum. It curates the very end of a line. Within its walls are the Dodo, the cuckoo clock, the number 9. The museum is, in itself, the last museum –'

'And the library,' Angela says, holding up her hand.

'Excuse me?' the guide says. Her smooth forehead twitches.

'The last library. That's in there too.'

Maggie, the guide, has long fingernails the colour of greenback beetles. They click as she flicks at the screen. 'That's on storey fourteen,' she says. 'Old exhibit. It's not interactive. Due to be shut.'

Angela's heart punches like a librarian's stamper. 'But we'll get there?' she asks.

Maggie's forehead almost creases. 'We'll have a quick look if there is time, though we are due at the winery at four and, if we are any later, will miss the complimentary tasting of the last Sancerre.'

Dad lets out a protesting snort and leans over to talk to his boss; his laugh sounds like rain in a tin bucket. He uses it when he's trying to get something out of a richer man. Mum reaches down and smoothes out Angela's fringe where it kicks out on the left side. 'We'll get you a souvenir,' she says. 'Why don't you play with those kids?'

Three kids sit on the top step, sharing a packet of Gruzzlers. The tall girl sees her watching, waves and beckons her over; the friendship bands hugging her arm jangle.

Angela walks over, biting her lower lip, hands balled deep into the pockets of her jacket. 'Hello,' she says, hoping her fringe behaves.

'Put this in the bin, would you?' the girl says, shoving the packet up Angela's sleeve.

Angela turns away. Their laughter bounces off the museum's shiny black walls.

'This way,' Maggie shouts over the heads of the group, marching up the steps and through the dark doors. The entrance hall is as tall as any building Angela has seen. It skies up, supported by columns of different centuries and last kinds, all standing on each other. Angela touches a Greek column that curls at the top like posh women's hair, on top of which is a red painted metal column from a railway station, then the dirty square column from a hospital waiting room.

'No touching,' Maggie shouts, swiping Angela's hand away. 'Right. Let's start with the last.

'How do you know it's the last one?' Angela asks.

'There are verifiable records and exhaustive studies and – we just do,' Maggie replies.

'But there might be another one left, or more. How can you verify if something doesn't exist? If you haven't seen it, it might.'

Maggie's eyes roll so much they must get dizzy. 'Let's move on, shall we?'

Stalking through corridors and vast rooms, Maggie chatters

away and pours out facts the way that, at dinner parties, Mum tops up glasses already full of acidic wine. Angela dawdles at the back of the group, feeling like one of the sandbags outside her house, heavying up with floodwater. Every last, lonely thing makes her want to smash the glass and grab the pen, the pacing badger and the handkerchief and let them go.

In one dark room, the last stained window leans against the wall. Even without light behind it the reds and blues and golds burn. She presses her fingertips to a diamond of green glass. It curves slightly outwards, like a tummy. A clammy hand clamps on her shoulder, yanks her away. The potato-faced security man, all tiny eyes and nose hair, pushes her out of the room. 'No touching,' he says.

Her mouth opens, closes again.

The stairs up to storey fourteen twist round and round. Angela pushes her way up to the front of the group, ducking under armpits and crawling through legs. One man has a blue umbrella where his right leg should be. A war wound, probably: maybe it opens up when it's going to rain.

Squeezing between two plump ladies, she sees it: the reason she came. The Last Library. Behind two walls of glass and a decompression chamber. Angela's breath seems stuck. She's researched it online, in arcane sites and planes, but to see the thick wooden doors with Greek symbols down the frame makes her grin.

'Come in, we haven't got long,' Maggie says, pushing Angela across the stone threshold onto the wooden floors.

The smell gets her first. Lemon polished wood, dusty cologne, and the faintest taint of burning, as if all the brains fired up by the books leave behind their smoke. Shelves reach up for the domed ceiling and shush hangs a canopy over them. And on the shelves, books: cheek to cheek, nestling together; inviting her to lean against the spines and shoulders; each one containing a world and people she can get involved with. Her mind is always full of stories, and now there are more outside her. She is home.

Reaching out to touch one, she sees a boy staring at a book open on a desk as if it were a fire and he were cold.

'Books,' Maggie says, looking at her gold watch, 'were made up of paper, a few of you may remember paper, and paper grew on trees, trees of course being bushes on stilts, if you can imagine that. They were grown by a kind of gardener, called an author.'

A loud cough comes from behind one of the shelves.

Maggie frowns. 'Anyway –'

'You can't tell them that, you stupid woman.' A tall woman steps out, holding a stack of books. She has pink-rimmed eyes and creased skin with soft white fuzz that makes Angela think of an elderly bespectacled mouse in a twin set, standing on many other mice.

Maggie gasps. Angela smiles.

'That is the most ridiculous nonsense. If you are going to make stuff up then at least make it magical,' the tall mouse lady says.

'Who are you?' Angela asks.

'I'm Hedda, the librarian. I used to be Head Librarian but now there are no other librarians I've lost my Head.'

'You're the Last Librarian!' Angela says, tugging at her sleeve.

'No,' Hedda says, 'I don't believe that.'

The glass doors shoosh open. Four men in white overalls come in holding mallets and sacks. One of them winks at Maggie and stands close to her, talking.

She nods and a flash of triumph passes across her face.

She looks at Hedda. 'We're in luck,' she says. 'You are about to see the last library being destroyed. Every last book will be incinerated. It's a rare event for the museum but they have to make way for other last things. That's progress.'

A whispering shush comes from shelves around the library. One of the books open on a table slams shut. Another sighs its pages. Apart from Angela, only Hedda and the boy seem to notice. He stares at Angela, eyes wide.

The men sweep books off the shelves into the sacks and swing the mallets at the shelves. Wood cracks and splinters. Angela runs up to one of the men and grabs his elbow. 'Stop it, stop it.' He peels her off and pushes her away.

'Don't make a scene, Angela,' Mum says.

More men arrive, with smooth faces and ties. They tick books off shelves and nod to each other.

Hedda shuffles up to Angela. 'Take these,' she says. Her voice squeaks like an opening door. 'You're the librarian now. Remember: magic. And that there are no such thing as last words.'

Angela feels her jacket pull downwards. Placing her hand in her pockets, she finds four, thin, shuddering books. She strokes their backs till they are still.

Hedda is talking to the boy now. His face freezes with his eyes at their widest. She winks at him, at Angela, gestures with her bristly eyebrows to the exit and then sits cross-legged on the floor, holding onto one of the desk legs. Two of the demolition men pull at her. She holds on and starts singing a low, lilting song that increases in volume and hangs in the air like the last word of a ghost story.

Angela walks out of the museum, hands on the books

to keep them quiet, waiting for alarms to sound around her. But they don't. The boy walks out with the ashen skin of burned books. He sits on the steps with his hands in his coat pockets.

'Come on, Angie,' Dad calls from the car.

Angela runs up to the boy. 'I'm at the top of the Trench Building. Number Not-Nine.'

He stares at her, then at his pockets. 'Oh,' he says.

Angela spends the next days in her room, opening the books, placing her fingers to the yellow pages, reading, living each story through, eating apple after apple core and occasionally thinking of how annoying that boy's answer was. 'Oh.' Huh. The books huddle next to each other, cooing like the birds in the communal gardens' dovecote.

Her parents come in to tell her they have received a screen from the Museum of Last Things, saying that some of the books have gone missing. 'We told them we wouldn't know anything about that. It must have been that mad librarian. Should be locked up, that one.'

'Like the things at the museum,' Angela says.

'Like you should be, in bed,' her mum replies.

Angela wakes, shaking, from her nap to the sound of banging on the door. She can hear her mum's surprised voice, and agreeing voice. Leaping up, she goes over to the windowsill and her little library, stacked next to each other. Two men burst into her room. They take her hands out from behind her back and snatch the books away.

The man with a shiny head eats crisps as he rips. Tears form in Angela's eyes as pages float down in pieces. He sweeps up the pages and tips them in the sack. Shoving his hand in, he pulls out four other books – the boy's books – and grins a crisp-gummed grin. Angela looks down and sees one torn piece of poetry by her shoe. She steps on it. The men do not notice, they are too busy grinning.

Angela sleeps with the piece under her pillow and dreams of feathers floating down like torn pages, settling on soil and swelling into swans.

Next morning, after toast and chrysanthemum jam, Angela runs out to the communal garden. Digging with her hands, she scoops out the earth and places the piece of paper in the hole. It folds over once, bowing to her.

'What you doing?' It's the boy, standing next to her, hands in his pockets.

'What do you think I'm doing?' Her face gets as red as the Little Red Book.

'I'm Tom, by the way.' He pulls a hand out of his pocket and in it is a crumpled piece of paper – a page from one of the books. Bending down, he places it with the other fragment and sprinkles on the soil.

'It won't work you know,' he says. But he watches.

She watches. He watches. They both watch at different times, sometimes with eyes that hope, sometimes with eyes that don't. Nothing happens apart from they both get tummy ache from eating apples and get cramp sitting cross-legged on the grass. After a couple of days, they lean against each other, first editions, and tell each other the stories they've been storing: new ones; old ones; stories that end badly; stories that do not end.

On the sixth day, the soil shifts. Angela watches as a hand reaches out of the earth, holding a book. The hand stretches out its soil-caked fingers and shoots into leaves; the leaves hold onto branches; each branch has a dozen or more books that breathe in and out, the branches to a trunk, the trunk to the earth. On the trunk, the knots are covered in open eyes.

Mrs Oldcastle from Number After-Not-Nine creaks out of her deckchair and walks over. 'Is that a book?' she asks pointing to one of the windfalls on the ground. She picks it up, puts on her glasses and dances a little dance. Angela has only ever seen her walk with a limp before but she scurries now, back to her room, smiling and muttering.

One by one, then in groups, first from the building – Mr Spedding, the Warden, the Eyebrow twins – then from the street, then from the outer towns, people came to get books. When they have read them, they come back and hand them in for another.

Angela and Tom sit by the library tree, handing out books, hearts stamped. 'Do you think they'll come for us?' she says.

Tom takes a page and plants it in the ground. He places a finger to his lips. 'Ssssh,' he says.

Leaves float down around them, like feathers and last words.

Contributors' Biographies

SOCRATES ADAMS lives in Manchester and works as a bookseller. His first novel, *Everything's Fine*, was published by Transmission Print in January 2012. He has had stories published in *Shoestring*, *Word Soup: Year One* and *Murmurations: An Anthology of Uncanny Stories About Birds*.

AK BENEDICT read English at Cambridge and studied creative writing at Sussex. She has composed film and TV soundtracks and has published short stories and poems in small journals. Her first novel, *The Beauty of Murder*, is due to be published in late 2012.

NEIL CAMPBELL has published two collections of stories, *Broken Doll* and *Pictures from Hopper*, and two chapbooks of poems, *Birds* and *Bugsworth Diary*. From Manchester, he lives in Northumberland, where he is studying for a PhD in the short story.

RAMSEY CAMPBELL is the author of numerous novels and short story collections. He has been described, by the *Oxford Companion to English Literature*, as 'Britain's most respected living horror writer'. He is the President of both the British Fantasy Society and the Society of Fantastic Films. He lives on Merseyside.

STELLA DUFFY has written twelve novels, ten plays and forty-five short stories. She won the 2002 CWA Short Story Dagger and has twice been named Stonewall Writer of the Year. In addition to her writing work, she is a theatre director and performer.

STUART EVERS writes about books for the *Guardian*, *Independent* and *Telegraph*. His fiction has appeared in *Prospect*, 3:*AM Magazine*, *Litro* and elsewhere. His first novel, *If This is Home*, is due to be published in July 2012. He lives in London.

JULIAN GOUGH was born in London, grew up in Ireland and now lives in Berlin. He is the author of the novels *Juno & Juliet* and *Jude*. His short story, 'The Orphan and the Mob', won the 2007 BBC Short Story Prize.

JOEL LANE was born in 1963 and lives in Birmingham. He is the author of the novels *From Blue to Black* and *The Blue Mask* as well as a novella and four collections, *The Earth Wire*, *The Lost District*, *The Terrible Changes* and the booklet *Do Not Pass Go*. He has also edited or co-edited three anthologies of short stories.

JO LLOYD, brought up in Wales, has won the Asham Short Story Award and the Willesden Herald International Short Story Prize. Her stories have appeared in *New Short Stories 3*, *Cut to the Bias* and *Riptide*. 'Tarnished Sorry Open' received a McGinnis-Ritchie Award from *Southwest Review* for the best fiction published in the magazine in 2011.

Award-winning poet and playwright JAKI MCCARRICK was born in London to Irish parents and educated at

Middlesex University and Trinity College, Dublin. Her story, 'The Visit', won the 2010 Wasafiri Short Fiction Prize.

JON MCGREGOR's first novel, *If Nobody Speaks of Remarkable Things*, was followed by *So Many Ways To Begin* and *Even The Dogs*. His short story collection, *This Isn't the Sort of Thing That Happens to Someone Like You*, was published in 2012.

ALISON MACLEOD is the author of two novels, *The Changeling* and *The Wave Theory of Angels*, and a short story collection, *Fifteen Modern Tales of Attraction*. She lives in Brighton and teaches creative writing at the University of Chichester.

DAN POWELL's short stories have appeared in *Staccato*, *Neon*, *Metazen* and elsewhere. His story, 'Half-mown Lawn', won the 2010 Yeovil Literary Prize for short fiction. Living in Germany, he teaches part-time while studying for a distance-learning MA in creative writing.

WILL SELF is the award-winning author of eight novels and as many short story collections. A broadcaster and journalist, in February 2012 he was made Professor of Contemporary Thought at London's Brunel University.

ROBERT SHEARMAN has published three collections – *Tiny Deaths, Love Songs for the Shy and Cynical, Everyone's Just So So Special*. An award-winning playwright, radio dramatist and *Doctor Who* screenwriter, he is currently resident writer at Edinburgh Napier University.

MICHAEL MARSHALL SMITH has published – under that name and as Michael Marshall and MM Smith – ten novels and four collections of short stories. Born in Knutsford, Cheshire, in 1965, he now lives in Santa Cruz, California.

HP TINKER is the author of the short story collection, *The Swank Bisexual Wine Bar of Modernity*. His stories have also appeared in *Dreams Never End*, *The Mammoth Book of Best British Crime*, *Bloody Vampires* and elsewhere.

JONATHAN TRIGELL's first novel, *Boy A*, won the John Llewellyn Rhys Prize and was adapted as a BAFTA award-winning television film. He has published two more novels, *Cham* and *Genus*. Born in 1974, he lives in Chamonix.

EMMA JANE UNSWORTH's short fiction has been published by Comma, *Prospect* and Redbeck Press. Her first novel, *Hungry, the Stars and Everything*, was published by the Hidden Gem Press in 2011.

JEANETTE WINTERSON was born in Manchester and brought up in Accrington. Her first novel, *Oranges Are Not the Only Fruit*, was published in 1985. She has since published numerous books and in 2006 was awarded an OBE for services to literature.

Acknowledgements

'Wide and Deep', copyright © Socrates Adams 2011, was first published online at *Metazen*, March 2011, and is reprinted by permission of the author.

'The Last Library', copyright © AK Benedict 2011, was first published online at *Paraxis* 02, and is reprinted by permission of the author.

'Sun on Prospect Street', copyright © Neil Campbell 2011, was first published in *Pictures From Hopper* (Salt) and is reprinted by permission of the publisher.

'The Room Beyond', copyright © Ramsey Campbell 2011, was first published in *Postscripts 24/25 – The New and Perfect Man*, ed Peter Crowther & Nick Gevers (PS Publishing), and is reprinted by permission of the author.

'To Brixton Beach', copyright © Stella Duffy 2011, was first broadcast on BBC Radio 4 and is printed here by permission of the author.

'What's in Swindon?', copyright © Stuart Evers 2011, was first published in *Ten Stories About Smoking* (Picador) and is reprinted by permission of the author.

'The Dark Space in the House in the House in the Garden at the Centre of the World', copyright © Robert Shearman 2011, was first published in *House of Fear*, ed Jonathan Oliver (Solaris), and is reprinted by permission of the author.

'Sad, Dark Thing', copyright © Michael Marshall Smith 2011, was first published in *A Book of Horrors*, ed Stephen Jones (Jo Fletcher Books), and is reprinted by permission of the author.

'Alice in Time & Space and Various Major Cities', copyright © HP Tinker 2011, was first published in *Ambit* 206 and is reprinted by permission of the author.

'Aperitifs With Mr Hemingway', copyright © Jonathan Trigell 2011, was first broadcast on *The Verb*, BBC Radio 3, and is printed here by permission of the author.

'I Arrive First', copyright © Emma Jane Unsworth 2011, was first published online at *Paraxis* 02, and is reprinted by permission of the author.

'All I Know About Gertrude Stein', copyright © Jeanette Winterson 2011, was first published in *Granta* 115 and is reproduced by permission of PFD (www.pfd.co.uk).